GUN TOWN

STACKS

GUN TOWN

JACKSON COLE

WHEELER
CHIVERS

This Large Print edition is published by Wheeler Publishing, Waterville, Maine, USA and by BBC Audiobooks Ltd, Bath, England.

Wheeler Publishing is an imprint of Thomson Gale, a part of The Thomson Corporation.

Wheeler is a trademark and used herein under license.

LIBRARY OF CONGRESS CATALOGING-IN-PUBLICATION DATA

Cole, Jackson.
   Gun town / by Jackson Cole. — Large print ed.
     p. cm. — (Wheeler Publishing large print western)
     ISBN-13: 978-1-59722-508-3 (softcover : alk. paper)
     ISBN-10: 1-59722-508-8 (softcover : alk. paper)
     1. Large type books. I. Title.
   PS3505.O2685G85 2007
   813'.52—dc22   2007002394

BRITISH LIBRARY CATALOGUING-IN-PUBLICATION DATA AVAILABLE

Published in 2007 in the U.S. by arrangement with
Golden West Literary Agency.
Published in 2007 in the U.K. by arrangement with
Golden West Literary Agency.

U.K. Hardcover: 978 1 405 64106 7 (Chivers Large Print)
U.K. Softcover: 978 1 405 64107 4 (Camden Large Print)

Printed in the United States of America on permanent paper
10 9 8 7 6 5 4 3 2 1

GUN TOWN

CHAPTER 1

Sitting his great golden sorrel, on the crest of a rise that seemed to drop down into a black void, Jim Hatfield gazed at a cluster of twinkling lights that were like stars fallen from their high estate.

Hatfield knew that those lights marked the site of the sprawling construction camp that was the rail end of the C & P line. Behind him, north and south stretched the ragged, craggy mass of the Diablo Hills, and into the granite breast of the range the railroad builders were tearing their way with sledge hammers and steam drills and giant powder. It was C & P's plan to cut a tunnel through the hills. To the north, nearly thirty miles distant, the M & K was also building a railroad, circling the northern tip of the hills in a vast, sweeping curve. The terrain to the north offered less construction difficulties, but the finished line would be many miles longer than the C & P route. Jaggers Dunn, the General Manager of the C & P, envisioned the time when those extra miles of haulage would work to the disadvantage of the M & K. Also, farther west, the M & K line would barely skirt the great valley through the very center of which the C & P would drive its fingers of steel. And this valley, now arid and inhospitable, its sands glaring in the sunlight, its dust pirouetting in a fantastic dance in the arms of the wind, Jaggers Dunn was confident would be the garden spot of the region when irrigation would pour life into this home of death.

As he gazed at the lights of the construction camp, Jim Hatfield, himself a trained engineer, thrilled at the courage of the men working to make their great dream come true.

"It's what Texas needs most," the tall Ranger mused, "men who believe in her, not only for what she is but also for what she will be."

Jim Hatfield was a legend throughout the Southwest. His exploits were discussed with an admiration almost amounting to awe wherever honest men got together; and he was cursed with fear and fury in outlaw circles.

Hatfield would have been much interested in a conversation that took place in a mahogany office in the state capital some months before between Crane Ballard, president of the M & K Railroad, and Archibald Watson, Chairman of the Committee on Corporations in the lower house of the Texas legislature.

Crane Ballard shook his fist in Arch Watson's face.

"As a legislator, you stink!" he declared savagely.

Watson seemed to cringe back from the angry railroad president. He threw up his plump hands in a fluttery, futile gesture of defense. He appeared abjectly fearful of physical violence. Ballard glared at him contemptuously.

A more observant man might have noted that Watson's little pig eyes, set deep in rolls of fat, were hard as marbles. His thick lips were drawn tightly against his stubby teeth. But Ballard was not a particularly observant man and at the moment his judgment was clouded by anger.

"Oh, I'm not going to hit you," he said. "I wouldn't dirty my hands on you, but I repeat, as a legislator you stink. Here you assure me that you have that infernal C & P extension bill bottled up in your committee and that it will not even reach the floor of the House. And what happens? When most of our men are absent and there's only a bare quorum on the floor, the proponents of the bill vote it out of committee and pass it, and you know damn well the C & P has the senate and the governor lined up in their favor. They'll get their franchise sure as hell!"

"Crane, you got no cause to be mad with me," Watson whined in the high-pitched piping voice so often characteristic of a fat man. "I handled my end of the deal. It was you who gave that barbecue and rally for the boys over to San Marcos, forty miles away. How was I to know the damned engine would break down and delay the special train till the boys couldn't get here in time to kill the bill?"

"That engine didn't break down, it was sabotaged — emery dust in the journal boxes," Ballard swore. "How was I to know —"

"Just what *I* was saying," interrupted Watson. "We were both outsmarted."

Ballard glared at his henchman but was visibly cooling. "I still think you stink," he growled, "but I guess recriminations are no good at this stage of the game. Jaggers Dunn and his railroad will get their franchise to build to Franklin and will buck us to the Pass and the Pacific, but the fight's just

10

started."

He rose to the full of his better than six feet, flexed his powerful arms, squared his broad shoulders, towering over the squat and rotund Watson. His mouth was a thin straight line above his long blue chin.

"Forget it," he said. "They outfoxed us this time, but I repeat, the fight's just started. Wait till they get to building their railroad, then watch the fireworks! But I don't want any more fool blunders from you. Slip up again and watch out, Arch Watson, watch out!"

Watson watched him leave the room, assured, arrogant. A vicious sneer twisted Watson's thick lips.

"Set up to be salty, eh?" he apostrophized the railroad president. "Uh-huh, plumb salty, but when the real business begins, your guts will turn to water!"

To New York, Chicago, and half a dozen Texas towns and cities, the telegraph ticked out the information that the C & P Extension bill had passed the lower house and would be through the Senate and signed by the Governor within twenty-four hours.

The news was also relayed to far-off El Paso County and to Ranger Post Headquarters there. Stern old Captain Bill McDowell shook his grizzled head.

"It means war," he told the clerk. "A hell-roarin' railroad war. The M & K bunch will stop at nothin'. There'll be folks pourin' in, and money spent like water. And every blasted owlhoot within a thousand miles will be swoopin' down on the section, on the lookout for pickin's. Reckon I'd better make a provision against that. Go get Jim Hatfield in a hurry."

And now the Lone Wolf was on the scene of strife and bloodshed, ready to take up the gage thrown down by the forces of evil.

Southwest of the Deleware Mountains, in Culberson and Hudspeth counties, is one of the most desolate, yet weirdly beautiful sections in Texas; a vast view of level reaches, gray-green with sage and greasewood, with stands of prickly pear, yucca and octillo. Streaks of blazing white gleam like hazy silver ribbons encircling shallow cups of turquoise where the salt-encrusted shores of salt lakes follow iregular curves of age-old death and dessication. Ragged peaks and sheer walls of rainbow coloring loom starkly against the sky. Deep, narrow canyons split the ridges, their mouths sultry cobalt in the sunshine, black onyx when the moonlight falls in a silver flood and the salt-impregnated sands are a ghastly white. It is a land of great distances, of greater loneliness, of legend and tradition where fact and fancy intertwine and the real and the unreal become one.

And across this land of story and of promise, the energy and genius of James G. "Jaggers" Dunn, empire builder, was uncoiling the steel ribbons of a railroad where cynics declared a railroad could not be built.

"But what of the Diablo Hills?" he was asked. "They lay athwart the route you have mapped out. You can't go over the Diablos."

"We'll go through 'em," Dunn replied. "They'll not stop us."

And gazing down from his ridge crest at the great construction camp, bustling and active even during the hours of darkness, Jim Hatfield was confident that the man of vision would go through the Diablos despite any obstruction in his path. Hatfield didn't stop to ponder the fact that it was he, Hatfield, who would have the chore of removing quite a few of the obstructions and that, without his help, the grand plans of the empire builder would come to naught.

In the blaze of a full moon riding high in the sky, Hatfield could see the gaunt buildings that housed the workers, the great store rooms, the shops and roundhouse. Farther to the south and east were the ramshackle structures of the town of Graham that had mushroomed in the wake of the road builders; a town of saloons, dance halls, gambling halls, stores, eating houses and other places of which the less said the better.

From the south, almost in line with where he sat his horse on the ridge crest, came the ceaseless chatter of the drills, the puffing of locomotives, the thud of mauls and the crash of steel on steel. The night shift was hard at it, for neither the construction camp nor Graham ever slept.

Hatfield turned in his saddle to glance back to where the trail, blue and silver in the moonlight, wound across the hills. He gazed for a moment, then turned back and gathered up the reins.

"Okay, Goldy," he said, "we might as well be ambling. Ought to be something to eat in that pueblo down there, and a helpin' of oats for you. We'll — good gosh almighty!"

One instant the construction camp lay bathed in the white moonilight. The next, the buildings were outlined in a reddish glare that paled the lights and seemed to quiver the stars. The hills rocked to a thunderous explosion. For a moment a pall of yellowish smoke hung over the camp site. Then it was shot through by soaring red flames. The landscape was bathed in a baleful sunset glow.

For a crawling moment, Hatfield stared at the holocaust below. Then his voice rang out, urgent, compelling.

"Hit the trail, feller," he shouted. "All hell's busted loose down there. This needs a mite of looking into!"

The great golden horse shot forward, his irons drumming the hard surface of the trail. He dropped plummet-like from the crest of the ridge and was almost instantly swallowed up by the shadows of the tall growth flanking the steep track. Leaning low in the saddle, Hatfield urged him on. From the direction of the construction camp sounded a stutter of shots.

The trail wound and zig-zagged, reached a wide bench and levelled off. Again it dropped dizzily downward. Then its steepness gradually decreased as it neared the foot of the slope. Directly ahead was a sharp bend, on either side of which the short chaparral formed a solid wall of ebony.

Above the drumming of Goldy's irons sounded another and a louder drumming. Hatfield's hand tightened on the bridle.

Around the bend bulged a group of racing horsemen packing the trail from one side to the other.

There was no room for Hatfield to swerve his mount. It was too late to pull up. The meeting was head on and disastrous for the Ranger. Despite his great weight and strength, Goldy was knocked off his legs by the crash of the impact. Down he went, kicking and squealing. Hatfield had barely time to jerk his feet from the stirrups and hurl himself sideways from the hull. He hit the ground with stunning force, rolled over and over in the dust.

From the charging group arose a chorus of yells and curses, then a blaze of gunfire. Bullets kicked dust into Hatfield's face, tore jagged holes in his shirt. One grazed his ribs like a white-hot iron. Another burned a streak across his cheek. Prone on the ground, at the edge of the trail, he jerked his guns and sent a stream of lead hissing toward his attackers.

There was a scream of agony. A shadowy figure whirled from a saddle and thudded onto the trail. Another man howled a curse and his gun dropped from a bullet smashed hand. Then the horses went drumming up the trail, their riders turning in the saddle to fling back a few wild shots.

Hatfield staggered erect, saying a number of things that wouldn't have sounded good in church. Goldy had already regained his footing and stood blowing and snorting.

"What in blazes —" Hatfield began. Then he made a grab for Goldy's bridle. "One side, feller," he shouted, "here come some more!"

Dragging the sorrel after him, he dove into the growth. Around the bend charged another compact band of riders. There was a wild clatter of sliding hoofs as they glimpsed the body lying in the trail and the riderless horse standing nearby, snorting and tossing its head.

"Look out!" roared a deep voice. "They went into the brush over there. I heard 'em!"

"No, they didn't!" another voice shouted. "You can hear 'em skalleyhootin' on ahead!"

"I tell you I heard 'em bust the bushes!" the first voice bellowed. "And there's one of 'em down. We must have plugged him."

Uncertain and divided, the group milled about the body and the frightened horse. Finally they dismounted, and approached the still form in the dust.

A voice rang out from the dark growth — "Elevate! You're covered!"

With yelps of alarm the group stiffened, caught in an unprepared huddle. They turned to face the growth.

There was a crashing report, a bawl of pain. A man who had stealthily reached toward his holster reeled back, pawing at his blood-streaming hand.

"Next one to make a move gets it dead center," warned the voice from the growth. "Up, I say!"

Hands shot up, high in the air. Their raging owners glared and muttered.

There was a crackling in the brush and the tall form of the Lone Wolf stepped into view. His level green eyes, now the color of wind-swept winter ice, surveyed the wrathful huddle.

"What's the big notion, anyhow?" Hatfield demanded harshly. "Can't a gent ride an open trail in this section without runnin' the risk of bein' downed by a bunch of gun-loco owlhoots? What's the big notion, I say? Speak up!"

"We ain't owlhoots!" a voice bellowed indignantly. "We're railroad guards."

"Isn't any railroad up here that I can see," Hatfield instantly countered. "What you doing up here? Was that part of your bunch that came along a minute ago? They nigh to busted my neck, and shot my clothes to pieces."

There followed a babble of explanation. The wrathful railroad guards apparently forgot all about the two long black guns menacing them. They waved their arms, gesticulated with their hands.

"Those M & K sidewinders! Blowed up the machine shop! Killed two fellers! After them!" were the coherent peaks above the clouds of confused bellowing.

Hatfield's lips twitched slightly. He holstered his guns. Nobody appeared to even notice the movement.

"Hold it!" Hatfield shouted at them. "I can't make head or tail out of this racket. Somebody do the talking, and the rest of you shut up. First let's take a look at that gent on the ground. I figure he's done for, but let's make sure."

The man on the ground was dead, all right, plugged plumb center. He was a rangy, hard-featured specimen with brindle hair, a scraggly bristle of beard on his chin, and a thin, bloodless gash of a mouth.

"I know this horned toad!" a big burly man suddenly shouted. "He's Sam Watkins, the hellion who killed poor Walt Sutherland in Graham last week. Walt never had a chance."

He whirled to face Hatfield. "Feller, did you get him?" he demanded.

"Well, I reckon I was the only gent hereabouts they were throwing lead at, and the only one to throw some back," Hatfield replied grimly.

The big man stuck out a huge paw. "Shake, feller," he said. "I'm Tobe Harness, in charge of the C & P railroad guards. Don't know who the hell you are or where you come from, but you sure did one fine chore. Put 'er there!"

A grin twitching the corners of his rather wide mouth, Hatfield "put 'er there," supplying his name as they shook. The big man's mighty fingers closed like a vise, but it was the railroad guard and not the Lone Wolf who winced slightly as their hands tightened together.

"Feller, you sure got some grip," he said, ruefully clasping and unclasping his numbed fingers as their hands fell apart.

"Tobe's sort of proud of the way he shakes hands, but it looks like for once he met a mite more than his match," Hatfield heard the man chuckle.

Tobe Harness evidently also heard the comment, for he grinned a trifle sheepishly. He jerked his thumb toward the dead man.

"That jigger," he explained for Hatfield's edification, "was a dealer in Ace Turner's Red Cow saloon over in Graham. He usually wore store clothes and went clean shaved. Reckon he let his whiskers grow for a few days so he'd be harder to spot when he was workin' with the bunch that blowed up the machine shop. Crane Ballard of the M & K has his men spotted everywhere. Walt Sutherland was a steel gang foreman and was playin' in the game Watkins was dealin'. An arg'ment started and Walt reached for his gun, but Watkins downed him before he could clear leather. And Turner's gunhands were right there to back up the play and swear Watkin's shot in self-defense."

"Not over much law in Graham, eh?" Hatfield remarked.

Harness shrugged. "Oh, they got a dep'ty sheriff stationed there, but he ain't no good. Bob Scarlet means well, but reckon he was sort of down in the cellar when they were handin' out brains. He ain't no match for Ballard and his crowd."

Harness turned to his men. "All right," he said, "a couple of you pack that hellion on his horse and bring him along. We'll take him to the dep'ty as a sort of exhibit. We might as well head back for the camp. The sidewinders got a head start now. Comin' along, feller?" he asked Hatfield.

"Figure to," he replied. "That was where I was headed for." He gave a clear whistle. There was a crashing in the brush and Goldy sidled onto the trail, glancing about with liquid, inquiring eyes.

"Golly, what a horse!" exclaimed Harness. He turned to Hatfield, lowered his voice.

"Cowhand, aren't you, feller?"

"Have been," Hatfield admitted.

"Well," said Harness, in a voice still lower, "I'm goin' to hand you a mite of good advice. Don't stop in town. Keep ridin'. When the word gets around that you did for that hellion slung across the horse's back, there'll be fifty salty reptiles on the prod for you. Fork that yaller horse and keep ridin'. That's the best advice I can give you."

"Much obliged," Hatfield replied. "Reckon it's good advice, all right, but I'm not taking it."

"Didn't figure you would," grunted Harness. "But you'd be showin' a heap sight more savvy if you did. All right, let's go."

Hatfield beckoned the man whose hand he had creased with a bullet. From his saddle pouch he took a roll of bandage and a pot of antiseptic ointment with which he deftly cared for the slight wound.

"That'll hold you," he said, giving the neat bandage a final pat. "Next time a gent has the drop on you, in this country, don't try to *snuk* your gun out. The next jigger might not miss and just skin your hand."

"Uh-huh," the guard agreed dryly, "the

next gent might *miss,* and —"

He rubbed his middle significantly to complete the implication.

Hatfield smiled slightly, but did not otherwise reply.

"All right, let's go," Tobe Harness repeated, swinging into the saddle. "We might as well get back to camp. Somethin' else might bust loose."

When they reached the camp site, the fire was under control, but the machine shop was a total loss. Harness swore bitterly as he surveyed the ruins.

"They're doin' everythin' they can to slow us up," he said. "The first road to get to Franklin is in line for some fat mail and express contracts. Also, about ten miles west of the hills is the only practicable pass through the Tonto range. If the M & K gets there first, they'll hold the pass and we'll have one hell of a time bustin' 'em loose. There'll be court orders and injunctions and hell knows what else. And all the while they'll be buildin' west. They'll lick us for sure if they get into the pass fust."

"You don't figure then they'll try to take possession of the pass and hold it till they get there?" Hatfield asked, although he very well knew the answer.

Harness shook his head. "Nope, they

wouldn't try that. Then they'd have the Rangers after 'em and the federal gov'ment and everything. But let 'em get in there first, and they can maintain they need the pass for sidings or a yard or what not. Of course they'd lose out that fight in the end, in the courts, but they'd have a case and be able to hold us up long enough to serve their purpose. Nope, as I see it, the first line to lay steel in the pass will be the winner of this shindig."

A crowd of several hundred was gathered around the smoking and flickering ruins. They were chiefly construction workers of the day shift, but Hatfield noted a sprinkling of mounted cowhands as well as a number of townsmen from Graham, a mile distant. Harness conversed with several men who were directing the fire-fighting operations. He led Hatfield to where two motionless figures lay beneath blankets.

"This is the worst of a row of this sort," he said bitterly. "We can build more machine shops, but we can't bring back these poor devils. They were the watchmen assigned to the shop. One with a knife stuck in his back, the other with his head busted open by an iron bar or somethin'. Both plumb done for. The murderin' skunks! Thank God the shop wasn't operatin' of nights yet, or hell knows how many would be dead. Though maybe they wouldn't have been able to pull it off with a force on the job. Lane Cardigan, the construction super, will give me hell over this. He'll figure the guards had ought to have prevented it. Well, we were outfoxed, that's all there is to it."

"Looks sort of like it might have been an inside job," Hatfield commented. "Perhaps that bunch ridin' away was just to turn you into a cold trail."

Harness looked startled. "Feller, you're smart," he said. "I never thought of that. Come to think of it, them ridin' gents did go skalleyhootin' off makin' a lot of noise right after the explosion. Naturally us fellers lit out after 'em."

"And gave the ones who really did the chore plenty of chance to get in the clear," Hatfield observed.

"Wouldn't be surprised if you're right," Harness admitted gloomily. "There's sure one smart hombre directin' things hereabouts. If we could just drop a loop on him —"

"Maybe you will," Hatfield interrupted. "He may have given you a line on him tonight."

"Maybe," Harness grunted, "but I sure don't see it, yet."

Hatfield said nothing more, but the furrow between his black brows deepened.

A horseman came cantering up. He waved a hand to Harness.

"Hello, Bob?" the guard captain greeted. "Hatfield, this is Dep'ty Bob Scarlet. Reckon he'll want to talk to you."

"Just got into town," the deputy said, dismounting. "Heard what had happened and figured I'd better ride over. What do you know, Tobe?"

Harness told him in terse sentences, including the part Hatfield played in the subsequent events. The deputy sheriff bent a searching glance on the Lone Wolf. He was an elderly man with a lined, kindly face and faded blue eyes that were, nevertheless, sharp enough. Hatfield had a feeling that Harness underestimated the peace officer's intelligence.

"Didn't happen to get a good look at any of 'em?" he asked.

Hatfield shook his head. "Nope," he replied, "they were all over me in a split second. Reckon they were as badly scared as I was, otherwise they would have shot better."

"From what Tobe just told me, you shot pretty well for a bad scared man," the deputy commented dryly. "Well, I reckon we'll hold an inquest tomorrow. We'll get the coroner over from Sierra, the county seat. Maybe Sheriff Benton will come over, too. You stick around, son," he told Hatfield. "We'll want your testimony. Figure to coil your twine in this section for a spell, or are you just passin' through?"

"Looks like an interestin' section," Hatfield replied.

"May hang around a spell, if I can tie onto a job."

"No trouble about that," Tobe Harness declared heartily. "You and me will have a talk later."

"I'll be gettin' back to town," the deputy said, mounting his horse. "See you tomorrow, Tobe."

Hatfield also mounted. "Ride along with you, if you don't mind," he said. "I feel the need of a surrounding of chuck and a place to pound my ear for a spell. Riding all last night."

"You can put your horse up in the stable where I keep mine," offered the deputy. "Old Seth Grey, who runs it, has some rooms over the stalls he rents out. Clean, and no bugs. Better than any of the roomin' houses in town, I'd say, and you can keep close to your horse like most cowhands like to be."

"That'll be fine," Hatfield accepted. "Much obliged."

As they rode to town at a leisurely pace, several groups of horsemen passed them, apparently with the same destination in mind.

"Cowhands," said the deputy, jerking his thumb toward the riders. "Big ranches to the east and north. The boys come to Graham for a bust. Other characters been comin' there too, the sort we could do without. They always show up when there's a gold strike or somethin'. And this railroad buildin' is about as near a gold strike as anything can be. The C & P and the M & K, up to the north, are biddin' high for labor. More money loose in this section than there ever was before, and loose money always makes for trouble."

Hatfield nodded sober agreement. As they rode through the outskirts of the construction town, he felt that Deputy Scarlet had stated the case mildly. From the main street they were approaching came a grumbling roar that increased in volume as they drew nearer. Boots pounded the board sidewalks. The irons of horses stirred the dust in the street to a cloud. From every window glared light. From over the swinging doors of the saloons came a whirling babble of conversation, the whine of fiddles, the strumming of guitars and snatches of song or what was intended for it. What sounded like a fight was going on farther down the street, to the accompaniment of much shouting and profanity.

The sheriff sighed wearily. "Never stops," he growled. "No use to try stoppin' it. You'd need an army to keep order. About all I can do is try to keep as many folks from gettin' killed as possible, and I don't have overmuch luck at even that. Okay, here's the stable, right down this alley. Then I reckon you'll want somethin' to eat. Ace Turner's Red Cow saloon serves about the best chuck in town. Can't recommend the joint for anythin' else, but they do put out a good meal."

Hatfield was satisfied with the looks of the stable and with the appearance of the little old man, a crippled former cowhand, who ran it. The little room offered him was also satisfactory.

"I'm headin' for my office to see if anything has busted loose while I was away," the deputy announced. "Drop in and see me when you're of a mind to. Just a little ways down from the Red Cow. There's a sign on the window. And here's the Red Cow. Chances are I'll show up before you're finished eatin'. Hope you get out alive."

A glance around the big saloon he entered a moment later caused Hatfield to feel that perhaps the sheriff's last remark was not as jocular as it might have been. Bartenders, dealers, lookout and other workers in the place had the look of hard men. Not particularly tame, either, were the customers that packed the long bar and crowded the gaming table. The lunch counter and the tables, provided for more leisurely customers, were sparsely occupied. Apparently eating was a secondary matter in the Red Cow.

Hatfield had to admit, however, that the deputy had not over-recommended the food. He was served with a prime surrounding of chuck to which he addressed himself with the energy of a man who has found good food scarce of late.

Standing at the far end of the bar was a very tall, broadshouldered and exceedingly handsome man whom Hatfield rightly guessed was Ace Turner, the owner. Turner was deep in conversation with a hard-faced man in dusty rangeland garb when Hatfield entered. He favored the Lone Wolf with a keen glance. Doubtless, Turner kept a close watch on his customers and devoted particular attention to new faces.

"I've a notion he needs to, from the looks

of this bunch," Hatfield mused.

Many of the drinkers and gamesters were undoubtedly railroad workers, judging from their clothes and general appearance. There were also a number of cowhands. And more than a sprinkling of gents who had the look of punchers, but who, Hatfield decided, were not, although perhaps the majority of them had been at one time or another. The girls on the dance floor were more than passably good looking. The dealers and the waiters were undoubtedly efficient and ready for anything.

"And most anything is liable to happen," Hatfield quickly decided.

Before Hatfield finished eating, Deputy Scarlet entered. He nodded to the Lone Wolf, and approached Ace Turner. Hatfield clearly overheard the conversation that ensued.

"Ain't seen that dealer of yours, Sam Watkins, around of late," remarked the deputy.

Ace Turner's cold eyes narrowed the merest trifle, but he replied in easy tones, "Nope, I let him go a few days back. Was gettin' a mite too light-fingered for his own good, and mine. Haven't seen anything of him since he left."

The deputy nodded. "See anything of that sidekick of his, Doc Horton?"

"Oh, he drops in now and then," Turner answered. "Between you and me, Scarlet, I could do without that killer. His sort makes trouble, sooner or later. Wonder you haven't dropped a loop on him before now."

"Uh-huh, I understand he's made trouble in here several times," the deputy returned dryly. "And each time, your dealers and barkeeps swore he acted in self-defense. And when he got in trouble over to Sierra, that buttery lawyer-politician, Arch Watson, bailed him out and got the charges dropped."

"Well, maybe he did act in self-defense in here," Turner admitted, his eyes narrowing again, "but just the same I could do without him. Trouble just nacherly followed that jigger around."

"And catches up with him plumb easy," grunted the deputy. "Uh-huh, he's a killer, all right, and one of the fastest gunhands I ever saw."

The subject changed, and after a few more observations, Scarlet left the saloon.

Jim Hatfield's black brows drew together slightly. He knew perfectly well that Deputy Scarlet knew that Sam Watkins was dead, and had the facts relative to his sudden demise. Hatfield wondered just what was behind this bit of by-play between Scarlet and Turner. He recalled that the deputy had spoken quite loudly, louder than was necessary, under the circumstances. The furrow between the Lone Wolf's brows deepened a little more.

After eating, Hatfield enjoyed a leisurely cigarette. Finally he pinched out the butt and stood up, preparatory to going to bed. At that moment a man pushed through the swinging doors and paused, glancing about as if in search of someone. Under his baleful glare, a sudden silence enveloped the room.

"Doc Horton! And he's lookin' for trouble!" Hatfield heard a man at a nearby table ejaculate hoarsely.

Horton was tall and thin, though broad-shouldered. His arms were abnormally long and hung loosely at his sides. His hands, also, were long with bony spatulate fingers. A heavy gun sagged low on his right thigh. Hatfield noted that the bottom of the holster was tied down.

Horton's face was arresting in appearance. It had a cadaverous look, the cheeks sunken, the cheek bones high, the skin stretched tightly over them. He had a long, cleft chin. The glitter of his eyes were like to the crawling fire in the heart of a black opal.

"Killer, all right, and plumb bad," was the

Lone Wolf's verdict.

Horton crossed the room with long, loose strides. He paused directly in front of the Ranger and only a few feet distant. He looked him up and down with sinister, unblinking eyes.

"Feller," he said, without preamble, "I'm a friend of Sam Watkins."

"That so?" Hatfield returned easily. "Aren't over particular, are you?"

Horton's jaw dropped. Hatfield heard somebody's breath catch sharply.

Horton appeared to recover himself. His bony face darkened.

"Yes," he said, his voice a lion's growl, "Sam *was* a friend of mine. I understand he got done in tonight — shot in the back."

"Reckon you got it straight about the first part, all right," Hatfield admitted, "but whoever told you was sort of mixed up as to his directions. The hole I saw in Watkins started in his breast bone."

"That ain't the way I heard it," Horton replied in menacing tones, "and I sure ain't takin' your word for it bein' different."

"Meaning," Hatfield returned easily, "that you're calling me a liar. Well, here's my answer to that!"

His left hand lashed out, the open palm catching Horton squarely across the mouth.

Horton went reeling back, blood spurting from his cut lips. He staggered, slammed into a table, turned a complete flip-flop and crashed to the floor. Hatfield stood watching him, his thumbs hooked over his double-cartridge belts and directly above the black butts of the long Colts sagging in their carefully worked and oiled cut-out holsters.

Horton came to his feet with a roar of rage. The flicker of his right hand to his holster was too swift for the eye to follow. But before the big gun half cleared leather, the room rocked to a shot.

Horton sagged back with a howl, and hit the floor again. This time he stayed there, blood pouring from his bullet smashed shoulder.

There was an instant of shocked silence, shattered by a second roar from Hatfield's long Colt. A bartender who had come up with a sawed-off shotgun went down again, minus the shotgun, yelling with pain and clutching at his broken arm. Hatfield's voice rang out, edged with steel —

"Anybody else? I aim to accommodate, gents!"

The grim promise was emphasized by the black muzzles of his guns, wisping smoke that weaved back and forth like the head of snakes prepared to strike, and seemingly singling out each and every occupant of the room for individual attention.

Ace Turner's shout stilled the rising tumult. "Hold it, everybody!" he thundered. "Curtis, what the hell did you horn into this for? It was a fair gun slingin' and Horton got the worse of it. Serves him right for comin' in here startin' a rukus. All right, some of you fellers, pack Horton and Curtis out of here and take 'em to the doctor."

He spoke with evident authority. The babble of rising voices lowered to a subdued murmur. Turner strode over to Hatfield who had holstered his guns and was calmly rolling a cigarette with the slim fingers of his left hand.

"Sorry, feller," Turner said. "I don't know what this is all about. Did Horton say Watkins is dead? Watkins used to deal for me."

"Reckon he didn't make any mistake as to that," Hatfield replied. "If he wasn't dead when I last saw him, some jigger with a spade will play a mighty mean trick on him about tomorrow."

"You killed him?"

"Well," Hatfield answered, "I can't say for sure. Maybe one of his owlhoot partners drilled him, but I was sure throwing lead in his direction when he left the hull."

"Feller, I don't want to be askin' questions," Turner said, "but would you mind tellin' me what this is all about? How come you got into a wring with Watkins?"

Hatfield told him, in a few terse sentences. Turner shook his head, and swore.

"I sure wish them two darn railroads would get together and stop their rowin'," he complained. "That sort of thing is bad for business. This town would be all right if it wasn't for the wringin' between the roads. She'd be salty, all right, like all construction towns of this sort, but there wouldn't always be the makin' of a real free-for-all like there is now. A feller never knows which way the pickle's goin' to squirt. Have a drink with me?"

Hatfield accepted the saloonkeeper's offer, and then headed for bed.

"Drop in again," Turner invited cordially. "Sorry you had the row with Horton, but maybe he'll cool down a mite after this. I've a notion he ain't feelin' so uppity about now."

The occupants of the saloon stared at Hatfield as he made his way out. There were shakings of heads, whispered comments.

"Wouldn't have believed any man livin' could have shaded Doc Horton that way," Hatfield heard said as he passed through the swinging doors. "Why, Horton didn't

37

even get his gun out. Gentlemen, that was shootin'!"

As Hatfield left the saloon he bumped into Deputy Scarlet who was hurrying across the street.

"I heard about it," said the deputy. "Feller, you've got yourself a rep'tation in this pueblo. Doc Horton has been sort of the big skookum he-wolf hereabouts for quite a spell. Had himself quite a name over in Tucson and Tombstone, Arizona, too, before that section got too hot to hold him and he had to pull out. Sure glad you came out of it like you did. I was scairt —"

Scarlet abruptly ceased speaking. Hatfield smiled slightly and completed the sentence for him —

"That Horton would do for me. Much obliged for the warning you gave me when you were talking to Turner."

"You got plenty of savvy, all right," Scarlet conceded. "I felt pretty sure you'd catch on. But I didn't figure Horton would come lookin' for you tonight, or I'd have stuck around. Somebody made it their business to get the word to him mighty fast. Wonder how he came to take it up like he did?"

Hatfield was wondering about that, too. Not for a minute did he believe Horton was motivated by revenge for the death of Watkins. The snake-eyed killer must have had a stronger reason for his obvious attempt at murder.

"That sort isn't friends wth anybody," the Lone Wolf told himself as he said goodnight to the deputy and headed for the stable. "I'm willing to bet a hatful of pesos that Watkins meant nothing to him. What is his game, anyhow?"

If Hatfield could have overheard a conversation between Ace Turner and the man in the dusty clothes who hurried into the saloon a short time afterward, he might have been considerably enlightened.

"How's Horton?" Turner asked anxiously as he led the dusty man to a table set apart in a corner.

"He ain't so good," the dusty man replied. "He won't do any gun throwin' for a couple of months, maybe more. He got a hard jolt."

"Uh-huh, a heap harder than it looked to be, I've a notion," Turner replied. "I think that big hellion busted more than his shoulder — busted his nerve, too. Horton has always set up to have the edge on any jigger he tackled. Now that he's found out he ain't, it won't do him any good. He ain't the sort to go up against odds. He won't be sure of himself after this."

"Folks said he was fastest jigger on the

draw in the whole southwest."

"Well, they ain't sayin' it now, not folks who were in here tonight. Vance, I don't like it. I'm plumb convinced now I was right when I told you I figured that big hellion was sent in here by the C & P. You get hold of Cooney soon as you leave here and tell him to hightail up to the M & K and tell Crane Ballard what happened. No, I don't like it."

"Hell, one jigger by hisself can't do over much," Vance scoffed.

"His sort can do plenty," Turner differed grimly. "Besides, that sort is usually tied up with a bunch. And if he's a fair to middlin' sample, there'll be hell."

"If he was sort of — got rid of," Vance remarked contemplatively.

"That would be fine!" Turner sneered. "But who's goin' to take over the chore, after Doc Horton fallin' down on it like he did tonight?"

Vance leaned closer. "There are other ways," he said softly. "I figured at the time it was a fool notion to have Horton come in and brace him that way. Oh, I know Horton is always itchin' to kill somebody, particular if he gets well paid for it, but that sort of thing is always too liable to slip up like it did tonight. That wouldn't be my way."

"Okay," Turner instantly countered, "go ahead and try your way, and I hope you have better luck than Horton did."

CHAPTER 2

Hatfield slept soundly, but just as the false dawn flitted across the sky like a pale and lonely ghost, he arose, slipped downstairs and got the rig on Goldy. He led the sorrel from the stable, mounted and rode swiftly toward the construction camp.

The light in the east was strengthening, but the prairie was still clothed in blue-purple shadows that crawled through the mist like living things just arousing from sleep.

For some moments Hatfield sat gazing at the fair scene spread before his eyes. Then he turned Goldy's head and rode slowly around the bend. Where the dynamiters had milled about on the trail he paused again. He dismounted and studied the multitude of prints. He exclaimed with satisfaction as he noted the mark of a shoe with a broken front calk. The defective iron provided a track that was as plain to the trained eyes of the Lone Wolf as a deliberately blazed trail would have been. He swung into the hull and rode on. The hoof marks topped the rise, continued down the far side of the sag. For another two miles they led on into the hills. Then abruptly they ceased.

Hatfield pulled up, and studied the ground. Almost instantly he saw where the horsemen had turned left from the trail. Scattered twigs and broken branches plainly showed the course they had followed. Hatfield sent Goldy into the brush, a look of satisfaction on his bronzed face.

A mile farther on the course began to veer from south to east. The marks showed purposeful riding, as if the dynamiters had a fixed objective in mind.

"Thought so," the Lone Wolf told Goldy. "They headed back to Graham. That's where they holed up. Thought it was sort of funny that after the explosion a mounted bunch would go skalleyhootin' off, raisin' blazes and attracting everybody's attention. The logical thing would have been for two or three jiggers to slip in under cover of the dark, lay out the watchmen, set the charges with a long fuse and then sneak off and be plumb in the clear when the dynamite let go. The hellions wanted to give the impression that the charges were set by a bunch from the M & K camp up to the north. The bunch Harness tailed was all set and waiting, and when the explosion went off, they hightailed. Fooled Harness, all right. He lit out after 'em pronto. The jiggers that really placed the charges ambled off at their leisure. The M & K, if the M & K was really responsible for what happened last night, must have the town salted plenty with their hands. Well, this little slip-up may make it interesting for some gents. Now my chore is to get back to town without giving anybody the lowdown as to where I've been."

Instinctively he turned in the saddle to gaze about. Abruptly he stiffened, his glance fixed on a dense clump of thicket to the rear and a little to one side. There was the crash of a shot. The tall form of the Lone Wolf hurtled sideways from the saddle, crashed through a tangle of growth and vanished from sight. Goldy charged forward, swerved into the chaparral and also disappeared.

For a long moment there was silence. Then a twig snapped, there was a rustling of branches. From the thicket to the rear a man rode, a man clad in dusty, sweat-streaked rangeland garb. With head thrust forward, he peered and listened, a cocked rifle at the ready. He spoke to his horse and the animal moved slowly forward, his rider intent and alert. At the spot where Hatfield had sat his horse the man pulled up, shooting quick glances in every direction.

"Now where in blazes did the hellion get to?" he muttered aloud.

He gave a yelp of alarm as a voice replied, "He's right here!"

Jim Hatfield stepped into view, gun in hand.

Convulsively, the man threw his rifle forward. There was the roar of a shot, a clang of metal striking metal. The rifle flew from the horseman's hands and crackled through the brush. The man himself sagged in his saddle, as though very weary. Slowly he toppled sideways and thudded to the ground.

"Damn!" exploded Hatfield, staring at the blue hole between the drygulcher's eyes, "that's just what I didn't want to do. I wanted the sidewinder to talk. The slug glanced off the rifle lock and drilled him dead center!"

Disgustedly he ejected the spent shell from his gun, replaced it with a fresh cartridge and holstered the weapon. He strode forward and gazed down into the dead face.

"Seems to me I saw this jigger someplace before, but darned if I can place where," he mused. "Wonder what he's got on him?"

Squatting beside the body, he began

methodically turning out the pockets, disclosing a miscellany of odds and ends of no significance. He paused as he drew forth a folded bit of paper. He opened it, stared at the cryptic wording it displayed.

In rude, cramped writing was a column of words —

Two beres
Six whiskeys
One mele

Below, in a bold, flowing hand, the single word —

"Roof"

Hatfield stared at the paper, shook his head. Finally, his eyes very thoughtful, he folded and carefully stowed it in an inside pocket. He studied the body a moment more, then dragged it into the brush and left it there.

"May puzzle the hellions a bit when he doesn't show up," he told himself.

Without difficulty he caught the dead man's horse which was standing patiently. He removed the rig and cast it into the brush.

"Reckon you can fend for yourself a while,

feller," he told the animal. "Sooner or later you'll end up on some spread or back where you come from."

Upon hearing his master's voice Goldy had poked his head from the bushes where he had taken refuge, a habit due to long training. He came trotting up the trail at Hatfield's call. The Ranger mounted and rode due south for several miles before he veered east. He circled the town and entered it from the east, riding directly to the stable and putting up his horse. Then he strolled down the valley, searching the ground with keen eyes. In an open space between two shacks he found evidence that a horse had recently stood there for some time.

"Thought so," he mused. "Smart jigger, all right, and with plenty of patience. Figured I'd be leaving the stable maybe before daylight. Stayed holed up here till I showed. Reckon it was too dark to take a shot at me when I left the stable, so he tailed me. Did a good chore, too. I never spotted him. Maybe he was just curious as to where I was heading, and when I turned off the trail he knew I was showing considerable interest in the movements of that bunch last night. Decided I'd better be put out of the way. Would have made a job of it, too, if I hadn't glimpsed the shine of his rifle barrel just as he pulled the trigger. Was touch and go, all right. I felt the wind of the slug as it went past. Uh-huh, it's a salty outfit, with plenty of savvy."

Hatfield ate his breakfast in the Red Cow saloon which at that hour was practically deserted. Ace Turner was not in evidence, doubtless sleeping.

After finishing his meal and smoking a cigarette, Hatfield repaired to the deputy's little office. Bob Scarlet was there, as was Tobe Harness and several of the railroad guards. Also present was a fat and pompous individual who was introduced as Sheriff Dick Benton. He regarded Hatfield with a slightly jaundiced eye and evidently with scant approval. A prosperous cattleman who had been elected to office, Hatfield decided. Certainly not an efficient type of peace officer, but honest enough, was the Lone Wolf's opinion.

"The sort of a jigger who makes mistakes and sticks by 'em," was his verdict as he shook the sheriff's hand, which was very moist.

The coroner, a rugged old frontier doctor with a brown face that did not move a muscle, was more cordial and gave Hatfield the impression of having plenty of wrinkles on his horns.

The coroner impanelled a jury which quickly brought in a typical cow country verdict, first 'lowing that Hatfield did a good chore on the hellion he downed and slipped up only in not doing in a few more. The two watchmen met their deaths at the hands of parties unknown and the sheriff was advised to run the hellions down as soon as possible. A surprising and completely unorthodox rider to the verdict congratulated Hatfield on busting Doc Horton's shoulder the night before but regretted that it might delay the deserved hanging of the darn nuisance.

Sheriff Benton sputtered his indignation at that concluding effort on the part of the jury, but Deputy Bob Scarlet chuckled, and the coroner's eyes developed a more lively twinkle. Tobe Harness guffawed out loud and was reminded by the sheriff to respect the dignity of the court.

"Benton's all right, but he takes himself a mite too seriously," Harness chuckled as he and Hatfield left the office together. "He owns the big Lazy B spread over to the northeast. Sort of retired from business a couple years back and got into politics."

"You talk as if you were familiar with the section," Hatfield observed.

"Reckon I'd oughta be," Harness returned. "Born and brought up in this section. Was a cowhand before I signed on with the railroad, a couple years back. Which brings me to what I wanted to talk to you about. Rec'lect you told me last night that you might stick around if you tied onto a job? How about signin' on as a guard with my bunch? I can fix it up with Cardigan, the big boss. It's considerable of a ridin' chore. We patrol from here over east for ten miles to where they're buildin' the big steel bridge across Horse River. Run the material trains across a temporary wooden trestle. That trestle gives trouble every time there's a hard rain up to the north. Been washed out twice already. They're havin' trouble with the bridge, too. Considerable of a buildin' chore, I take it. But Sime Price, the engineer in charge over there, is a good man and he'll lick it yet. Well, what you say?"

Hatfield considered briefly. The notion fitted in with his plans.

"You draw down considerable better pay than for cow handlin'," Harness urged.

"Okay," Hatfield agreed. "Reckon you've hired yourself a hand."

"Fine!" applauded Harness. "We'll go over to the cut and see Cardigan right away. I'll get my horse."

Lane Cardigan, the construction superintendent and engineer in charge, proved to be a slender man, bowed in the shoulders. He had a finely shaped head and good features, but a slightly nervous mouth. His hands were slim and beautifully shaped. He had a competent look about him which was modified by the unexpected twitching of his lips.

"A good man, but never completely sure of himself. Liable to be swayed by a more forceful character," Hatfield analyzed the engineer.

After surveying the work in progress, Hatfield decided that no matter what he might lack, Cardigan knew his business.

The engineer certified the hiring of Hatfield as a guard, without argument.

"I rely on your judgment in such matters," he told Tobe Harness. He bent an admiring glance on the Lone Wolf's towering form and broad shoulders.

"Tobe is pretty good at sizing men up," he remarked with a smile, adding, "You're sure sizable enough, Hatfield. Must be about four inches over six feet, aren't you?"

"About that," Hatfield agreed, smiling in turn to display even teeth startlingly white in his bronzed face.

"Okay," Cardigan reiterated. "I'll tell the clerk to put you on the payroll. Harness will acquaint you with your duties."

"Cardigan is a nice feller," Harness said as the engineer departed to attend to his multitudinous duties. "I like him better than Sime Price, his assistant, who's in charge over to the bridge. Price is salty and sort of ringy, but he sure gets things done. He makes his boys hop. You can report for work in the mornin', Hatfield; I'll put you on the patrol and you can ride over to the bridge and back. That bridge is a sort of trouble spot, or so we figure. If the hellions should pull somethin' over there, it would hold us up bad. We have enough trouble as it is with that darn trestle."

Hatfield nodded. He was watching the drills drive into the face of the rock to widen the cut.

"It's quite a chore, all right," he commented.

"Sure is," Harness agreed. "And look there." He gestured toward a beetling cliff that rose directly ahead, in its base a dark opening. "That's the tunnel. It'll be nigh onto a mile long, one of the longest ever druv, I reckon. They're almost through. It's a chore, but when it's finished it will save miles and miles of haulage, and that'll mean plenty later on when the freight begins pilin' up. Old Jaggers Dunn knows what he's about, all right."

Hatfield nodded emphatically. He had had dealings with Jaggers Dunn in the past and realized to the full that the old empire builder usually knew what he was about.

Leaving Harness, Hatfield rode back to town. He dropped in at the Red Cow for something to eat. Ace Turner, his back to the door, was busy at the far end of the bar. Hatfield walked up quietly behind him.

"Howdy, Turner?" he remarked in affable tones.

Ace Turner whirled at the sound of Hatfield's voice. In his eyes was something very much like consternation as he gazed up at the Lone Wolf.

"Just wanted to buy a return for that drink you treated me to last night," Hatfield explained cordially.

Turner recovered his composure. "Why — why, it isn't necessary, but if you feel that way about it, okay," he accepted.

As they sipped their drinks, Hatfield conversed pleasantly. Turner's answers were rather distraught. He kept glancing toward the door.

"Expecting somebody?" Hatfield asked cheerfully.

"Why — why, yes," Turner replied. "A feller promised to meet me here about now.

Don't seem to see anythin' of him, though."

"Maybe he got — delayed," Hatfield observed. "Well, figure to have a surroundin'. Join me?"

"I — got somethin' to attend to," Turner declined. As Hatfield sat down at a table, Turner said something to his head bartender in low tones and left the saloon. Hatfield smiled slightly. His green eyes were cold. For Jim Hatfield had remembered where he saw the man in the dusty, sweat-streaked clothes whose dead body lay stiffening in the bushes south of the hill trail.

He was the man who had conversed earnestly with Ace Turner and then left the saloon shortly before Doc Horton put in an appearance looking for trouble.

CHAPTER 3

Hatfield rode east the following morning. At the last moment, Tobe Harness elected to accompany him.

"They're havin' trouble over to the trestle and I want a look at it," Harness explained. "Water started comin' down bad last night. Must have been a big storm up to the north."

They rode past the big assembling yard that was being built just north of Graham and continued along the right-of-way. From time to time they passed gangs ballasting ties or grading for the double-track where the steel would soon be laid. At first, long trains of materials rumbled by, but as they progressed, there were no more. Strings of empties, however, headed east.

"They're havin' trouble with that darn trestle, all right," Harness grumbled. "Looks like all traffic is held up."

As they rode, Harness paid very little attention to the surrounding country, but Hatfield's eyes were everywhere, noting the movements of birds, of little animals, probing thickets, ridges and clumps of chimney rocks. He was very thoughtful and replied to Harness largely in monosyllables.

When they sighted the incompleted upper span of the bridge, Harness rose in his stirrups and gazed ahead.

"Uh-huh, I thought so," he said. "Look at them strings of empties lined up. They can't get across the trestle. Damn!"

Suddenly there was a sparkle of light crescenting through the air and a clang of metal on stone. Harness' horse had cast a left hind shoe. Harness swore. "But it don't matter," he added, "I can get another put on back at the camp. Have to take it easy on the way back, though. Don't want to lame the crit-ter."

As they drew near the river, they saw that a swarm of workmen were working franti-cally to bolster the supporting piers of the long trestle.

"Water's gettin' under 'em and washing the supports away," Harness said. "It's mighty like quicksand down there. They've had trouble aplenty anchoring the piers for the bridge. Can't seem to make anything hold. Sime Price is fit to be tied over that. He says the field men who run the surveyin' lines across here were plumb loco and handed him a purty nigh impossible chore. But if he can't do it, nobody can. That's what Cardigan says, and I reckon he ought to know. He's left the whole business in Price's hands. Price is, or so I've been told, a specialist on bridge buildin'. Cardigan felt he was mighty lucky to get him, I heard him say once."

"Cardigan hired Price, then?"

"Uh-huh, that's right. Reckon Cardigan was sort of lucky to get the big job here. The gent Old Man Dunn sent out here to run the shebang, a feller named Barnes, got hisself killed in a premature dynamite let-go and Cardigan fell into the job."

Hatfield nodded, thoughtfully, but did not

comment. His eyes were fixed on the incompleted steel structure several hundred yards below the trestle.

A man came climbing up the muddy, slippery bank, cursing as he moved. He was a big man, almost as tall as Hatfield, and of a heavier build. He had a square, blocky face dominated by hard blue eyes. His expression was arrogant and overbearng. His mouth was a tight line that cut straight across his face like the scar of an ill-healed knife wound. Competence and self-satisfaction seemed to ooze from him. He uttered a rumbling shout as his eyes fell on the two horsemen.

"You're just the feller I want to see, Harness," he said as he paused, breathing hard, on the lip of the bank. "I been trying to get through to the camp for the past hour but somethin's wrong with the blankety-blank wire and I can't make connections. You hightail back to the camp and tell Cardigan to rush every available man here pronto. If we don't get help in a hurry, this damn trestle is going out again!"

Harness hesitated, glancing at the shoeless hoof of his horse.

"You can ride my horse," Hatfield instantly offered. "He'll let you fork him when I tell him it's all right."

"That's fine of you, Hatfield," Harness exclaimed. "I couldn't make any time with my critter, and yours looks to be plenty fast. I'll be back in a jiffy."

Hatfield unforked and spoke a word to Goldy, who glanced rather questioningly at Harness but offered no objections when the big guard captain swung into the saddle.

Harness departed at a fast gallop. Sime Price, the engineer, gazed after him a moment, then turned his attention to the river.

"As if I didn't have enough trouble, this had to happen," he rumbled. "I don't know where all that darn water's coming from. Must have been a mighty bad rain farther north we didn't hear about. I don't understand it."

Hatfield didn't understand it, either. His keen eyes had noted something that the engineer had apparently overlooked. The water of the turbulent river was strangely clear for flood water. He started to mention the fact to Price, but the engineer was already sliding back down the bank to the scene of operations below.

After staring at the river for a moment, Hatfield turned and walked slowly downstream toward the bridge where work had been abandoned in favor of the sudden emergency at the trestle. For a long time he stood gazing at the uncompleted project, and as he gazed, his black brows drew together. After a while he walked back upstream. When Price reappeared a few minutes later, Hatfield made no mention of the peculiar condition of the flood water that had attracted his attention.

Price was still swearing over everything in general. He ceased abruptly, however, at the clatter of a horse's irons on the trail. He and Hatfield turned around and saw, to their astonishment, Goldy pounding toward them, stirrups flapping, split reins trailing. His saddle was empty.

"What in blazes —" began Price.

Hatfield's face had suddenly set in bleak lines. He seized the reins as Goldy jolted to a halt beside him. The sorrel was blowing hard but not, Hatfield instantly saw, from fatigue. He was affected by fright and excitement.

"Where you going?" Price demanded as Hatfield swung into the saddle and turned Goldy's head.

"To find out what happened to Harness," the Ranger replied.

"You figure he got bucked off?" Price shouted as Goldy's hoofs pounded the trail.

"I hope so," Hatfield flung back over his shoulder and was gone.

Mile after mile, Hatfield rode at top speed, anxiously scanning the trail ahead, and at the same time mechanically taking careful stock of his surroundings. He had covered perhaps five miles when he flashed through a grove and around a bend. The trail straightened out and he saw, perhaps five hundreds yards ahead, something lying motionless in the dust of the trail. As he drew near, it resolved into the body of a man. A few minutes later, Hatfield swung down beside what was left of Tobe Harness.

Harness lay on his face. There was a blue hole in his right temple. The whole left side of his head had been blown away where the flattened slug emerged.

Grimly, Hatfield gazed about. On all sides was open prairie, but to the right, nearly four hundred yards distant, was a clump of chaparral. The Ranger's gaze centered on the bristle of growth. His face set in lines of pain.

For Jim Hatfield realized that when he loaned Tobe Harness his golden horse, he had unwittingly sent the big, jovial guard captain to his death.

"They were after me," he muttered, his voice hard and metallic. "They spotted Goldy, knew him for my horse. They couldn't have distinguished features at that distance and Tobe was a tall man. The snake-blooded hellions! Hell, why couldn't it have been me coming along! I might have spotted the sidewinders."

Bitterly, he regretted not having gone himself.

Doubtless Harness had saved him from death, but the Lone Wolf's thoughts did not dwell on that. He only regretted that the guard captain had been called upon to make the sacrifice.

"But there'll be somebody along soon to open the Gate for you, feller, or I'm a heap mistaken," he grimly promised Tobe Harness as he swung into the saddle and rode toward the ominous thicket, his watchful eyes cold as frosted steel.

At the edge of the growth, Hatfield dismounted. He pushed his way into the thicket, glancing keenly about. Something glinting on the damp ground caught his eye. He stooped and picked up an empty rifle cartridge.

"That did it, all right," he deduced. "Here's the marks of the hellion's boot heels, deep in the soft, black earth, and the skinned patch on this limb is where he rested his rifle barrel. Over there is where his horse was tied. Wonder if I can trail the hellion?"

He examined the empty cartridge with care, a sudden glow in his green eyes. He carefully stowed it in a safe pocket. Then retrieving Goldy and mounting, he set out to follow the faint tracks on the grass, barely discernible marks that were nevertheless plain enough for the hawk-eyes of the Lone Wolf.

But the tracks almost immediately swerved to the travelled trail, where they were swallowed up amid other hoof prints.

"Headed straight for town," the Ranger muttered. "Maybe somebody saw him pass. Try and find out about that later."

He returned to where Harness lay, picked up the limp and heavy body without apparent effort and draped it over Goldy's withers. He remounted and rode for town at a fast pace.

From time to time he passed track workers or graders who dropped their work and stared at the grim burden. To each group he shouted a question. The answers he got were practically the same —

"Uh-huh, a feller rode past on a brown horse, about an hour back. Sort of tall feller with black whiskers. Nope, didn't know him. Don't rec'lect ever seein' him before."

Hatfield pushed Goldy as fast as he could, but he had no hope of overtaking the drygulcher, barring some unforeseen accident. The hellion had a head start. He would hole up in Graham, mingle with the crowd and be safe.

"Almost looks like he wanted to be seen riding to town," the Ranger mused, his eyes thoughtful.

Hatfield reached the construction camp. Men came running to him, crying questions. He passed Harness' body down to them.

"Tell you about it later," he replied briefly. "Got to find Cardigan pronto."

He located the engineer at the tunnel mouth and in a few terse sentences acquainted him with what had happened and relayed Price's message.

Cardigan went white. "My God!" he gulped. "Where will it all end? This is terrible. Yes, yes, I'll send a gang to the bridge as fast as an engine can get them there. Poor Tobe! He was a fine fellow and utterly dependable. I don't know who I'll find to replace him. I can't —"

He paused abruptly, staring at the Ranger. "Hatfield," he said, "you are new on this job, but Harness thought mighty well of you and you look dependable to me. I'm going to promote you to captain of the guards if you'll take the job."

"I'll take it," Hatfield replied, "on one condition."

"What's that?"

"That I be allowed to handle the chore my own way without interference from anybody. If I'm to be range boss of the outfit, I intend to run it as I see best."

Cardigan hesitated, gazing up at him. Hatfield looked forcefully at the engineer's face.

"All right," Cardigan said, with a shrug, "I've a notion you can handle it without any advice from me. You're on your own. Do whatever you think best. I don't see how you can make things worse than they are, anyhow."

"Okay," Hatfield answered, gathering up his reins.

"Where you going?" Cardigan asked.

"To town," Hatfield replied. "Bob Scarlet must know about what happened. And I want to see if I can spot a jigger forkin' a brown horse."

Cardigan gazed at the Lone Wolf's bleak face and terrible eyes. He stared after him as he rode off.

"Somehow or other, I've a notion that jigger forkin' a brown horse," he remarked aloud, unconsciously simulating the Ranger's way of speaking, "that jigger forkin' the brown horse is in for big trouble. And I wouldn't be in his shoes for the whole C & P system!"

The lines in Bob Scarlet's face seemed to have deepened when Hatfield finished recounting what had happened on the river trail. He shook his grizzled head sadly.

"Poor old Tobe," he said, "he was a right hombre if there ever was one. Him and me worked together on the Diamond H. This is what always happens in a row like this rukus between the two railroads. Sooner or later things get out of hand. Crane Ballard of the M & K is a hard man, but I don't believe he would countenance a thing like what happened today."

"You can't play with mud and not expect to get some of it on you," Hatfield replied. "Ballard shook his dogs off the leash and it looks like some of them turned out to be the hydrophobia brand. In a thing like this, there's always opportunity for the owlhoot breed."

Scarlet nodded agreement. "I'll send word to the sheriff," he said. "Benton liked Harness even though Tobe had a habit of pokin' fun at him. He'll feel bad about this. Chances are he'll be here tomorrow."

Hatfield left the office and repaired to the Red Cow for something to eat. Ace Turner was there when he entered the saloon, standing at the end of the bar as usual. Hatfield gave him a keen glance, and as he did, his brows drew together slightly.

Turner was talking to a very fat man whose fleshy face was dominated by hard, blue eyes. Turner nodded to the Ranger. The fat man shot a glance in Hatfield's direction, his agate eyes glittering.

As Hatfield sat down and gave his order, Turner and the other man strolled over to the table.

"Hatfield, this is Arch Watson, who represents Culberson County in the legislature," Turner introduced his companion. "I was just telling him you'd taken a job with the railroad guards."

Watson held out a moist, fleshy hand, but when their grips closed, Hatfield felt that there was steely strength under the pudgy fingers. And doubtless despite his appearance, Watson was quite muscular.

"Glad to know you, Hatfield," the legislator greeted pompously. "Glad to know you. Glad you've signed on with the road. We need men like you to enforce the law in this turbulent section."

After a few more remarks, Turner and Watson returned to the end of the bar and conversed together in low tones. No mention was made of the death of Tobe Harness, and Hatfield did not see fit to discuss the matter. Apparently the news had not yet got around.

After finishing his meal, Hatfield spent the rest of the afternoon and evening getting better acquainted with the men with whom he was to work. He found the guards a likeable lot but rather ordinary so far as intelligence went. They were bitter about the death of the former captain, their wrath directed against the M & K and its operators. Apparently they did not resent Hatfield's elevation to the captaincy. He anticipated no trouble with them.

Later, Hatfield contacted Cardigan. The engineer was worried about conditions at the river.

"It's already holding us up here," he said. "They're out of steel and ties at the yard. The stuff has to keep moving to accommodate our needs here. I sure hope they get that trestle anchored by morning."

Hatfield regarded the engineer curiously. "How long since you been over to the bridge?" he asked suddenly.

"Not recently," Cardigan replied. "Mr. Price is in charge there. He is an experienced and capable bridge man, and I am not. I am a mining engineer, primarily, and of course this tunnel work is right in my line, but I've never had any bridge experience. Naturally, I am familiar with the basic principles of the work, but it is not my line. I don't have to worry about it, however, so long as Price is on the job."

Hatfield nodded, but did not comment. "Has Mr. Dunn been over here lately?" he asked.

Cardigan shook his head. "No, he is in Europe, or on his way back. He hasn't been here since just about the time the bridge building started. We were already at work on the cut and the tunnel, of course, but there was no hurry about the bridge, at the time. The temporary trestle takes care of material needs for the project. I'm beginning to worry about that bridge, though. If they keep having trouble with the water, it might hold up the whole project. Can't run heavy freight and passenger trains across the trestle. Too risky."

Hatfield nodded. He already knew that.

The first streak of light the following morning found Hatfield in the saddle, riding eastward. When he reached the river, he saw that the water was still high. It had not receded an inch during the night. However, it was no higher. The river ran a steady stream that gnawed persistently at its banks and continually threatened to undermine the trestle supports. Gangs of men were busy there, shoring and strengthening. Work on the great steel bridge had for the time been abandoned.

Price was not in evidence when Hatfield appeared. He did not seek to contact the engineer. After watching the work for a few minutes, he turned Goldy and rode back the way he had come. Once out of sight of the river, however, he turned the sorrel's head north and left the trail. He veered slightly to the east and several miles above the site of the bridge, he saw the river again. Reaching the bank, he followed its winding course. He had covered some fifteen miles when he pulled up abruptly with an exclamation. For several minutes he sat staring toward where the large creek ran out of the north, its course paralleling Horse River for a considerable distance, then turning sharply to the west and vanishing into the mouth of a canyon.

Hatfield surveyed the terrain with his keen eyes. He fixed his gaze upon the brush-clad summit of a rise a quarter of a mile away, and held it there for some moments. Then he turned Goldy around and rode back the way he had come. He looked back over his shoulder and before the rise was out of sight, he saw a horseman slip out of the brush and ride north at a fast pace. Hatfield nodded to himself and sent Goldy toward the construction camp at top speed.

Chapter 4

"No wonder that river is full of water," Hatfield told Cardigan, several hours later. "Up to the north, fifteen miles or so above the bridge, there's a big creek, almost as big as Horse River. It runs close to the river for quite a ways before turning west. Well, the hellions dammed that creek, put a channel through the ridge between the creek and the river, and turned the course of the creek. Now it's emptying its water into Horse River. Smart trick, all right. Somebody has plenty of savvy."

Cardigan swore in astonishment and wrath. "What in blazes are we going to do about it?" he sputtered.

"Send a gang of workmen up there, rip out that dam and turn the creek back into its original bed," Hatfield answered instantly. "Then post a guard there to make sure they don't try it again. Where the dam and the channel are now is the only spot where it would be possible to pull such a chore. The ridge broadens and is higher to the north."

"You think they might build the dam up again?" Cardigan asked.

"What I'm thinking about," Hatfield replied, "is what might occur to some smart jigger who'd see what could really be done there if it was handled right."

"What's that?"

"If they had built their dam a few feet higher and backed up the creek, they would have given *us* something to think about," Hatfield replied. "That creek runs out of the north between two ridges, with a deep channel between. They could have easily gotten a head of water that would have taken the trestle out, and along with it the work that has been done on the bridge, as if it were so much matchwood. All they would have needed to do, after the channel to the river was dug, was blow the dam and let her rip. Lucky for the C & P they didn't think of it, but they might. We'll take no chances."

Cardigan shook his head and swore. "How did you catch onto it?" he asked.

"From the water in the river at the trestle," Hatfield replied. "Although the river was swollen to almost twice its normal volume, the water was perfectly clear. No mud, no floating debris, as would inevitably have been present if the water coming down were flood water caused by heavy rains farther north. It was that way when I first saw it, yesterday. It was the same this morning, although the water had not fallen an inch. It looked almighty funny, so I took me a little ride to find out why, and did."

Cardigan gave the Lone Wolf an admiring glance.

"Hatfield," he said with conviction, "you should have been an engineer instead of a cowboy.

"Wonder why Price didn't notice what you did, the color of the water, I mean," Cardigan remarked suddenly.

"Reckon he was sort of busy," Hatfield replied dryly. "Well, *we'd* better get busy. Load up light wagons with men and tools. I'll guide them up there by the shortest route. Try and have everything ready by the time I get back here. I'm riding to town to see Bob Scarlet. Got a notion about something."

He did not wait to explain the "notion" but headed for Graham at a fast pace. In Scarlet's office, he explained to the deputy what had happened and described the terrain.

"What I want to know is," he concluded, "is that open range up there?"

"Why, no," Scarlet replied. "That's part of

Sheriff Benton's Lazy B spread. I know the place well. You want me to ride up there with you, Hatfield?"

"Isn't necessary," Hatfield repled easily, "but there's one thing I would like you to do. I'd like the loan of a horse. Figure Goldy needs a mite of rest."

Scarlet glanced out the window at the superb sorrel standing quietly with dragging reins, and looked slightly puzzled. Goldy certainly did not appear in need of leisure.

"Okay," he said. "Tell Seth Gray to let you have that dun in the far stall."

An hour later, Hatfield, forking the deputy's big gray horse, rode north by east at the head of a string of wagons loaded with workmen, tools and a quantity of staple provisions. Three of the railroad guards rode with him. They were armed with rifles and sixguns.

"You boys will have to stick around up there for a spell," Hatfield told them. "We'll build you a shelter, and I'll arrange for reliefs to take over the chore from time to time. I don't reckon I need to tell you to keep your eyes skun, after the things that have happened hereabouts of late, but if you don't you're liable to plumb lose interest in everything."

The guards understood the significance of

the warning and their faces set in grim lines.

A mile below where he had spotted the dam and the channel, Hatfield halted the wagons behind a ridge.

"You fellers keep an eye on things here," he ordered the guards. "I'm riding on alone to scout around a mite.

"Here's where you do your chore, feller," he told the gray horse. "If that jigger I saw hightail out of the brush this morning did what I figured he would, they'll be on the lookout for a hombre forking a sorrel, not a dun. As it is, maybe they'll take me for a brakes riding cowpoke."

A few minutes later he topped a rise and the diverted creek lay below and a half mile or so away.

"Thought so," he muttered as he cantered toward the stream.

Standing beside the roughly built dam were three men with rifles in their hands. They watched the Ranger intently as he neared them. Hatfield waved a hand and paused on the edge of the brimming channel and a little below the dam. He dismounted and allowed his horse to drink. Meanwhile he curiously eyed the men and the dam.

After the horse had slaked his thirst, Hatfield let the split reins fall to the ground and permitted the animal to graze. He strolled toward the three men.

"Howdy," he greeted. "Don't aim to be too curious, but what in blazes are you gents doin'?"

The foremost of the three, a big, bearded, rough-looking fellow eyed him suspiciously.

"Aim to pan for gold in the crik bed," he replied gruffly. "Turned the water so we could get at the gravel."

Hatfield nodded in understanding and moved a little nearer.

"Figure there's gold there?" he asked.

"Uh-huh," the man replied. "Figure it's worth givin' a whirl."

Hatfield shook his head. "Never knew of gold bein' found in this section," he said, taking another step forward. He was now as close to the man who held the rifle across his breast as Jim Hatfield ever needed to be to a man who might make a threatening move.

"Reckon there's lots of things you don't know, cowboy," the man returned.

"Reckon that's so," Hatfield admitted. "By the way," he asked cheerfully, "do you know anything about minin' law?"

The other's suspicion appeared to increase. "What you mean?" he asked.

"I mean," Hatfield replied, "that this is

private property you're on, part of the Lazy B holdings. You can't prospect owned land without authority from the owner."

The man glared. He shifted the rifle significantly. "Right here's all the authority I need," he growled truculently. "Now you get the hell away from here and 'tend to your own business."

Hatfield's hand shot out and jerked the rifle from the other's grasp. With a single wrench of his slim hands he snapped the stock off short. The ruined weapon dropped to the ground. Hatfield's steely fingers fastened on the man's shirt front. Before he could open his mouth to yell, he was hurled back violently against his companions, knocking both off balance. They scrambled, staggered, froze grotesquely in strained, awkward positions. They were gazing into the yawning muzzles of two rock-steady black guns that just "happened" in Hatfield's hands.

"All right," the Lone Wolf told them, his voice like to steel grating on ice, "drop those long guns, pronto!"

The rifles thudded to the ground. Their owners glared.

"Now your belts," Hatfield continued. "Unbuckle them and let them drop. Careful, don't make any mistake, or you won't have time to make another."

The raging trio obeyed. There was nothing else for them to do. Hatfield nodded as the belts and holsters joined the rifles on the ground.

"I see your horses are over there by the brush," he remarked. "Fork 'em and hightail back to M & K headquarters, and tell Crane Ballard his trick was trumped."

The bearded leader opened his mouth to speak, but thought better of it. He clamped his lips tight and slouched after his companions who were already mounting their horses with speed. All three glared rage and hatred at Hatfield and rode off. Hatfield watched them till they vanished over a rise. Then he gathered up the two whole rifles and the belts. He mounted the gray and rode back to the waiting wagons.

"All right," he ordered, "get 'em moving. Everything's clear."

He tossed the armload of weapons into the nearest wagon. "You boys come along and we'll ride on ahead," he told the guards, who were staring at the hardware Hatfield tossed into the wagon.

"What in blazes?" one demanded. "Where'd them irons come from?"

"Some fellers dropped 'em up there," Hatfield returned easily. "Come on, let's go."

The guard stared at him, shook his head and refrained from further questions. But when they reached the dam and dismouted, the same guard picked up the two sections of the broken rifle Hatfield had left lying there.

"Sure a lot of careless jiggers hereabouts," he remarked dryly.

"Throw good guns away, bust 'em up, and everything. Or rather," he revised, his eyes hard on the Lone Wolf, "I'd say they're mighty careful hellions. Uh-huh, plumb careful. Don't notice any *careless* gents layin' around with their toes turned up!"

After making sure that the work of removing the dam and filling in the channel was progressing satisfactorily, Hatfield headed back to the construction camp. The three guards silently followed him with their eyes.

"You know," one remarked, "I've got a feelin' I've seen that big jigger somewhere before, or heard about somebody like him. Can't quite figure it out, though."

"If I didn't know better," another returned dryly, "I'd say he's Wyatt Earp, Doc Holliday and Buckskin Frank Leslie all shoved into one skin. Wouldn't be surprised if he is!"

Upon reaching town, Hatfield paused at the telegraph office. He wrote out a cryptic message that caused the operator, sworn to secrecy by the rules of his company, to regard him with decided interest.

The message read —

"Guard captain here has only a limited authority."

It was signed "J. J. Hatfield" and was addressed to "James G. Dunn, General Manager, C & P Railroad, New York."

"There should be an answer by tomorrow," he told the operator. "Hold it for me."

Before eating, Hatfield stopped at the deputy sheriff's office. He found Sheriff Benton there, also the corpulent lawyer, Arch Watson. Also, somewhat to his surprise, Sime Price, the bridge engineer.

"I brought Sime back with me when I was over to the bridge today," Scarlet explained. "Figured he'd ought to be here for the inquest tomorrow. We'll hold it around noon."

Hatfield nodded. Sheriff Benton asked a number of questions relative to the death of Harness, most of them, in Hatfield's opinion, quite irrelevant. The interview did not heighten his estimate of the sheriff's intelligence.

"By the way," Watson put in pompously,

"who was the last person to see Harness alive?"

Hatfield let his gaze rest on the lawyer's face. The corners of his mouth twitched slightly.

"Well, suh," he drawled, "if we knew that, I reckon we'd be pretty well on the way to a hanging."

Deputy Scarlet chuckled, and even Price, who for some reason looked nervous and ill at ease, glanced at the lawyer and grinned.

Watson flushed. His hard little eyes glittered.

"I don't mean the man who shot him," he snapped. "I mean who did he contact last, so far as is known?"

"I reckon Mr. Price and myself were the last persons to speak with him, if that's what you mean," Hatfield replied.

"That's right," Price nodded. "Hatfield and I watched him ride away."

"Hmmm!" said Watson, rubbing the third and lowest section of his triple chin.

Scarlet shot the lawyer a disgusted glance. "I talked with those graders on the way back, Hatfield," he said. "They agreed with what you told me. A jigger forkin' a brown horse, a tall, black-whiskered feller, rode the trail toward Graham what must have been a very short time after Harness was downed. Couldn't get much of a description of him from them, for naturally there was no reason for 'em to more than notice his passing. One told me he wore overalls."

"That helps a lot," snorted Sheriff Benton. "About nine out of ten workin' cowhands in this section wear overalls."

Scarlet nodded. "That's so," he agreed, "which just tends to the notion that the feller was either a cowhand or was makin' to look like one. Of course we don't know he was responsible for the killin', but I'd sure like to give him a good once-over."

"You think the killer shot from that thicket you spoke of?" Watson asked Hatfield.

"Well," the Lone Wolf replied, "somebody was sure holed up there mighty recent. You could see where he tied his horse. The marks of his boots were plain in the soft earth, and there was a skinned place on a limb that looked mighty like a rifle barrel had been rested on it. And from right there was a clear view of the trail, about four hundred yards distant."

Hatfield made no mention of having picked up the empty rifle cartridge, which, at that moment, was carefully stowed in his pocket.

"Good shootin', all right," Scarlet commented. "Four hundred yards, and a movin' target!"

After some more desultory talk, Arch Watson left the office, Sime Price accompanying him.

Bob Scarlet gazed after the departing pair.

"That damn lawyer gives me a pain in the seat of the pants," he said. "He ought to choke on his fat."

"Now, now, Bob," protested Sheriff Benton. "Watson is all right. He's done as much for the Party in the past twenty years as any man in this section."

Which vindication of Mr. Watson ended the conversation in a disgusted snort from the deputy.

Hatfield saw Watson later when he dropped into the Red Cow for something to eat. The lawyer was at the end of the bar, talking in low tones with Price and Ace Turner.

Shortly afterward, however, Price and the lawyer left the saloon. Ace Turner busied himself at the bar, passing occasionally through a door directly behind which he usually stood, a door that Hatfield knew led to a back room Turner used as an office. As Turner passed back and forth, Hatfield glimpsed an iron safe, a desk, and other things. He noted that Turner always locked the door upon leaving the room.

Hatfield ate slowly. After finishing his meal, he smoked several cigarettes in a leisurely manner. Finally he pinched out a final butt, paid his bill and left the saloon. He strolled carelessly along the street, turned a corner, and quickened his pace. He entered an alley that ran back of the Red Cow, a very dark alley faced by blank walls. He stole forward cautiously, seeing the glow of a lighted window. A moment later he was peering into Ace Turner's office.

The room was deserted. The light from the desk lamp showed something that instantly centered Hatfield's attention. It was a short barrelled rifle standing in a corner.

Hatfield tried the window. As he expected, it was fastened down. He drew his knife and began cutting a notch in the base of the frame. A few minutes later he thrust the barrel of one of his guns into the notch and exerted a steady prying pressure.

There was a sharp snap as a catch broke. The window sash lifted slightly from the sill. Hatfield listened a moment then carefully raised the window and climbed into the room. He glided to where the rifle stood and seized the weapon. As he turned to retrace his steps the door knob rattled.

Hatfield leaped forward as the door swung open. A sweep of the rifle barrel hurled the lamp to the floor and extinguished it even as Ace Turner bounded into the room with a shout.

Turner was outlined against the light. Hatfield was in the dark. He lashed out with his left hand and knocked Turner sprawling. Before the half-stunned saloonkeeper could scramble to his feet, Hatfield was through the window and racing up the alley. Behind, there were sounds of wild yelling.

Hatfield whisked out of the alley mouth into a dimly lighted street. At top speed he turned another corner, and another. Then he slowed down, chuckling to himself. He circled around the town and reached his room in the livery stable. He covered the single window, lighted a lamp and examined the rifle. From his pocket he drew the exploded cartridge shell he picked up in the thicket from which Tobe Harness was shot. His eyes were coldly gray as he slid the shell into the breech of the rifle.

"Thought so," he exclaimed with satisfaction. "A thirty-thirty shell and a thirty-thirty rifle. An unusual calibre for this section. Uh-huh, and this gun has been fired recently. Turner neglected to clean it. Well, his little slip-ups may end by him slipping his neck into a noose. No certain proof as yet, but something to go on. And when he misses this saddle gun from his office, I've a notion he'll do a mite of worrying, and a worrying jigger is liable to make more slips."

He pried up a floor board and concealed the rifle under it. Then he went to bed and slept soundly.

CHAPTER 5

Hatfield was in the saddle again at dawn. He rode east till he reached the site of the bridge. The water in the river was at a normal level once more and workmen were busy on the uncompleted structure. Hatfield dismounted and walked out onto the span. Below, men were busy working on the massive center pier, the pier that had refused to stay in place.

Hatfield watched the operations for some time, his brows drawing together. He turned to stare up-river to where the water foamed around a sharp bend.

A man came climbing up the latticework of timbers that rose from the pier. He was a big man with a beefy red face, hot blue eyes and red hair. He seemed to be in a bad temper. He eyed Hatfield inquiringly. The Lone Wolf introduced himself.

"The new guard captain, eh?" the man nodded. "I'm Maloney, the stone-work boss. Glad to know ye."

Hatfield gave him a careful once-over. Maloney glared down at the unfinished pier, and spat.

"You don't seem satisfied with things down there," Hatfield observed.

Maloney grunted. "I'm not," he replied shortly.

"Know anything about bridge building?" Hatfield asked casually.

Maloney glared. "I've been at it for thirty years and better, worked all over the world at it," he growled. "I reckon I should know somethin' about it."

"Well," Hatfield said, "then why don't you put your knowledge into practice."

Maloney jumped. He glared at the Lone Wolf, but Hatfield read something very like apprehension in his blue eyes.

"What do ye mean?" he demanded.

"You know very well what I mean, Maloney," Hatfield returned quietly, his gaze hard on the other's face.

Maloney tried to meet the Ranger's steady eyes, but his own eyes slid aside. He shuffled his feet, fumbled with his huge red hands. Finally he looked up defiantly.

"I'm obeyin' orders," he said.

"So I figured," Hatfield nodded. "Getting some mighty funny orders, aren't you?"

"Damned funny!" Maloney growled. Abruptly, suspicion filmed his eyes.

"Who the devil are ye?" he demanded.

"I told you," Hatfield replied, "the captain of the guards."

"Yis, I heard ye say that," Maloney conceded, "but ye're asking some pretty queer questions for a guard captain and a feller what looks to be a cowboy."

"And you're giving some queer answers, or, rather, no answers at all," Hatfield instantly countered.

"I need me job," Maloney replied sullenly.

"You're liable to be out of one if it's proved you have a hand in what's going on here," Hatfield said, his voice suddenly hard.

"I told ye I'm obeyin' orders," Maloney repeated.

"Who's giving the orders?"

"Ye know very well who's givin' 'em — Mister Price."

"Price an engineer?"

"A darn good one."

"You mean, a damned *smart* one."

"Maybe the better word," Maloney conceded. Abruptly he raised his eyes to meet Hatfield squarely.

"I don't know who ye be, sor," he said,

"but I'm beginnin' to think ye're consider-able more than just a guard captain. Yis, I know what's goin' on here — what mon of my experience wouldn't — but I'll give ye my word for whatever ye think it's worth, that I don't know why. I been doin' what I'm told to do, but I'll tell ye straight, I don't like it."

"Doesn't make sense, eh?"

"It's worse than doesn't make sense," Ma-loney growled. "It's doin' over and over work that just might as well not be done. If ye're what I'm figgerin' ye are, ye know them piers won't never hold."

"Yes, I know that," Hatfield nodded. He studied the man, and decided he was hon-est.

"Maloney," he said suddenly, "I'm giving you a clean bill. I believe you wear a straight brand. When the time comes, I hope I'll find I was right."

"Ye'll find out just that, sor," Maloney declared grimly. "I'm matherin' sick and disgusted with what I'm doin' here, but a gang boss ain't in a position to tell the engineer in charge where he's wrong. All it would git me is me papers."

Hatfield nodded. "You can tell him when the right time comes, and it'll get your papers, all right, papers you'll be glad to show," he said. He held out his hand.

Maloney hesitated, wiped the mud off his own, on his overalls, and gripped Hatfield's slim fingers.

"It'll be matherin' foine to be workin' for a *man* again," he said.

"And forget about this talk, till the time comes," Hatfield cautioned.

"I've done forgot it already, sor," Maloney assured him.

The inquest over, Tobe Harness' body was productive of no results other than general agreement that Harness had been murdered. After the verdict was rendered, Hatfield headed for the telegraph office. There he found an answer to his telegram awaiting him. With a disgusted oath, he read —

"Mr. Dunn on high seas. Message will be handed him at the earliest possible moment."

(signed) Wainwright, Secretary

Morosely, the Lone Wolf mounted his horse and rode to the construction camp.

"Delay!" he growled to himself, "and every hour counts. Let a real flood come down that infernal river and thousands and thousands of dollars worth of steel will go plop! And the work will be held up indefinitely. Sure wish I could be sure of one thing — is Cardigan just stupid? Looks that way, but still there's no telling."

He pondered the matter, recalling that according to the story told by Tobe Harness, Cardigan was in charge of operations as the result of an accident, the death of his superior, to whom the chore had been assigned by Jaggers Dunn. He wished he had questioned Harness more fully as to the death of Barnes, the original engineer in charge. A premature dynamite explosion, Harness said. But had the explosion been accidental? Or had somebody plotted to get rid of Barnes and supplant him with Cardigan? Cardigan knew tunnel work, of that Hatfield was assured, but he was not a strong character.

"And maybe Sime Price was eased in on him without Cardigan knowing what was in the wind," the Ranger reasoned. "That might be the explanation. Wish I was sure."

Hatfield made the rounds to see that his men were on the job. He had drastically altered the disposition of the guards. Now all trails entering the camp or approaching the construction work were guarded. Only legitimate workers were allowed to enter. Strangers were barred.

"You've got five hundred men to watch as

it is," Hatfield told his subordinates. "That's more than enough, without mavericks straying around."

There had been some grumbling in the beginning, but a few words from the new captain and a glance from his level green eyes quickly silenced the objectors.

Hatfield had also stationed a guard force at the trestle across Horse River. His men shook their heads over this, and discussed it among themselves.

"He's in for a row with Price," one declared. "You know what Price told Tobe Harness, that he didn't need any help runnin' things at the bridge and he'd do his own policin'. Price is goin' to raise hell about this when he gets back from town!"

"Uh-huh," another agreed, "but Cardigan is the big boss, and I understand he gave Hatfield a free hand."

"Yes," replied the first speaker, "but Price will jump Cardigan, too. And I've a notion Cardigan is sort of scairt of him."

"Could be, but one thing is sure for certain, Hatfield ain't scairt of him, or of anything else that walks, creeps or flies. If Price bucks him, he'll get his comeuppance. And don't forget what Hatfield said: If he found us fellers weren't on the job over there every minute, he wouldn't like it. Me, I don't figure to do anything that big hellion don't like. Remember that happened to Doc Horton. Doc tried to do something Hatfield didn't like, and he's still in the hospital and if he's got good sense, he'll stay there, at least till Hatfield trails his rope out of the section."

"Uh-huh," nodded the other, who like his companion was a former cowhand. "Uh-huh, he's a *muy malo hombre,* all right."

"Yep, a very bad jigger, but when he smiles at you, he's about the most likeable feller I ever met. He's a man to ride the river with, all right."

"Plumb certain," agreed the other guard, paying Hatfield the highest compliment the cow country has to offer.

Hatfield found everything as it should be. He stabled Goldy and walked into the cut, pausing at the tunnel mouth. He learned that Cardigan was somewhere inside the bore. For several minutes he stood watching the water gurgle in the ditches — the job was a wet one — then he entered the tunnel.

Inside all was thunderous noise and orderly confusion. Follow-up gangs were busy widening the bore to accommodate double trackage. The main tunnel, of single-track width, was driving ahead at top speed. The roar of the drills, the thud of hammers and the intermittent chatter of a huge steam shovel vibrated the rock walls. Just beyond where the tunnel narrowed, a locomotive stood hissing and panting, coupled to a line of dump cars. The fumes from its stack made Hatfield cough, despite the blowers that sucked out the foul air and drew in a fresh current.

The glare of the lamps cast contrasting shadows and highlights on the sweating bare arms and shoulders of the brawny hard-rock men who plied their shovels and their ponderous bars and outlined lean faces like bronze medallions.

Hatfield strode on to where the great advancing steel shield protected the workers from falls of rock or earth. Here, where the drills bit unceasingly into the granite breast of the hills, he found Cardigan, superintending operations.

The engineer shouted a greeting, his voice barely audible in the uproar. Hatfield nodded reply and stood watching the steely attack on the rock wall that stubbornly resisted the drills.

Cardigan batted the water from his hat and wrung some from the dripping sleeves of his overall jumper.

"One of the wettest jobs I ever handled,"

he shouted.

Hatfield sniffed the air. "Seems there are fumes coming in here," he called back.

"That's right," Cardigan replied. "Copperas water here, and sulphur. Gets mighty bad at times. Without the blowers we couldn't carry on for an hour."

Hatfield nodded sober agreement to this. He knew how deadly the gas can be, arising from sulphur beds dampened by acid mineral water.

"The day is liable to come when the sulphur in this section is worth plenty," he remarked. "Hit much of it?"

"Just some shallow pocket deposits," Cardigan replied, "but you're right. There are apt to be great beds underlying this desert country somewhere. I've heard that the Louisiana deposits are gradually petering out. Texas is likely to become the great sulphur producing state, sooner or later."

The locomotive's stack boomed, sending up a cloud of stifled smoke. The long line of loaded dump cars began rumbling past. And abruptly, the activity in the bore diminished, then ceased altogether. The chatter of the drills was stilled. Men began trooping past, headed for the outside. The gurgling of the water in the ditches sounded loud in the sudden stillness. Three powder men were busy tamping dynamite into the drill holes for the evening blow before the night shift took over.

"As soon as that engine gets back with the car of new drills and other tools, we'll fire the blasts," Cardigan said. "We'll ride the engine out."

Some fifteen or twenty minutes passed and the chugging of the approaching locomotive boomed in the tunnel. With a screeching of brakes the material car halted some distance down the bore where it would be safe from chance flying rocks when the powder let go.

"Well," said Cardigan, "reckon we might as well shoot. Light 'em — *Good God Almighty!*"

The tunnel rocked and shivered to a thunderous roar followed by a terrific grinding and rumbling and crashing. The acetylene lights jumped and flickered. The whine of the blowers stopped abruptly. Up the tunnel boiled a swirling dust cloud, through which sounded the frightened yells of the engine crew.

"What in hell!" bellowed Cardigan.

The pad of running feet sounded. The engineer, fireman and brakeman leaped out of the dust cloud, eyes wild, faces white.

"The roof!" gasped the hogger. "The

whole damn thing came down right in front of the engine!"

A ghastly silence followed this announcement. It was broken by Hatfield's quiet voice —

"Let the dust settle a mite and we'll go see how bad it is."

It proved to be bad enough. From the floor to the cracked and shattered roof extended a solid wall of splintered stone. Hatfield's lips pursed in a soundless whistle as he surveyed it.

"How in blazes could I have overlooked a weak spot in that infernal roof?" Cardigan raved. "I'd have staked my life on it being solid."

"Looks sort of like you did — and lost," one of the powder men remarked with grisly humor.

Hatfield was sniffing the air. "Smell anything?" he asked casually.

Cardigan wrinkled his nostrils. "Dynamite fumes?" he exclaimed. "What in hell —"

"Looks sort of like somebody misplaced a stick of powder," Hatfield said.

"Misplaced, hell!" Cardigan exploded. "No misplaced stick would have brought that roof down. It was set, deliberately set, to hold us up, like everything else they've been doing."

"Or to get a new engineer," Hatfield drawled with a little grim humor of his own. "If much of the roof is down, the C & P is mighty liable to need one."

Gasps followed this statement. "The — the boys will dig us out," Cardigan said, uncertainly.

"They'd better work fast," Hatfield replied. "Look how the water is rising. The fall has dammed it. And that isn't all. Notice the change in the air already? The blowers are busted. Those sulphur fumes are liable to do for us before the water gets a chance. Listen!"

He held up his hand for silence. Straining their ears, the imprisoned group could hear faintly a confused shouting on the other side of the rock barrier.

"Might be worse," Hatfield said. "Hear that they're already at work."

A tiny clicking sound seeped through the mass of stone. Picks and bars and sledges were tearing into the fall.

"John Lang, my head foreman, is out there," Cardigan said. "He's a good man with years of experience at this kind of thing. He'll understand and do everything he can."

"Reckon we might as well start to work on this side," Hatfield suggested. "Plenty of tools here. No, the drills are no good. The lines are busted, of course. The drills are dead. Picks and bars and sledges. Let's go."

"Think we can risk a blow?" asked Cardigan. "Plenty of powder back here."

Hatfield glanced at the shattered roof and shook his head. "No," he decided. "Too big a chance of bringing on another and worse fall. Powder is out."

Sloshing in water that was already ankle deep, Ranger, engineer, train crew and powder men ripped and tore at the stubborn stone that walled them in. Without the blowers, the heat in the bore was terrific. They streamed sweat. Their hearts pounded, their breath came in hoarse gasps. Soon all were coughing spasmodically. The sulphur fumes were thickening. Very shortly the air would be unbearable.

But the clicking and shouting beyond the barrier was steadily growing louder. The rescuers were working at frantic speed. Experienced hard rock men, they knew the terrible danger threatening their imprisoned fellows.

"Can't stand much more of this," Hatfield panted, trying to get some air into his aching lungs.

Even as he spoke, one of the powder men slumped forward and splashed into the water. Hatfield stooped and raised him. Cradling the limp form in his arms, he staggered up the gallery with it to where the water was shallower and the unconscious man would be safe from drowning for the moment.

"That damn engine isn't helping," gasped Cardigan as Hatfield rejoined the workers. "The smoke is darn near as bad as the fumes. Look out, there goes Mike! Carry him back up the bore."

A second powder man had joined his unconscious companion. Hatfield stepped back, his face set in bleak lines.

"All right," he told the others, "back up the bore. We're doing no good here. Back up and lie down against the end wall. Last longer that way."

As the others began staggering up the tunnel, Hatfield stood listening intently.

"They're getting close," he said to Cardigan who had lingered beside him. "I've a notion that mess isn't over thick now. But it'll take too long for them to bust through. We'll all be done for before they make it. I'm going to take a chance on something. Can't very well make things worse."

"What?" gulped the other.

"I'm going to try and knock a hole through that mess with the engine," Hatfield replied. "Can get a pretty good run from the head of the bore. Should be able to hit it a hefty lick."

"And kill yourself!" gasped Cardigan.

"Going to be done in anyhow," Hatfield replied. "At least, that way will be quick. Come on, I'll shove that car back to the head of the tunnel. Uncouple it when we get there."

He swarmed up the steps and into the engine cab. "You say your foreman out there is a smart jigger?" he called down to Cardigan. "Maybe I can get a signal over to him. Don't want to kill somebody if I do bust through."

He seized the whistle cord and blew three evenly spaced blasts. He waited a moment and repeated the back-up signal, and repeated it a third time.

"They've stopped hammering," Cardigan called up as the whistle's uproar ceased. "They've caught on."

"Chances are they figure we've decided to risk a blow," Hatfield replied. "All right, grab on, and we'll shove back to the head of the bore." He threw the reverse bar over, cracked the throttle, opening the cylinder cocks at the same instant.

The stack grumbled. Watery steam hissed from the open cocks. The locomotive moved back, wheels grinding on the rails. To the end of the steel, Hatfield shoved the loaded car.

"All right, cut her loose," he called as he closed the throttle and applied the air brakes.

"All set," Cardigan shouted a moment later. Hatfield threw the reverse lever to forward position, cracked the throttle. The locomotive moved ahead. The couplers opened with a clang, releasing the material car. Hatfield twirled the sand blowers wide open, sending streams of sand gushing onto the rails in front of the great drivers.

"Here we go!" he shouted to Cardigan. "So long, feller!"

"Good luck!" the engineer yelled.

Hatfield pulled back on the throttle bar. The drivers gripped the sanded rails. The engine gained speed. Hatfield slammed the reverse bar clear down in the corner and jerked the throtttle wide open.

The exhaust roared. The flanges screamed on the rails. The ponderous locomotive shot forward like an unleashed demon. Booming, thundering, pouring forth clouds of black smoke and clots of fire, it rushed toward the barrier of fallen stone.

Hatfield saw the splintered mass leap into the glaring beam of the headlight. He flattened his body against the hot boilerhead, held on with both hands.

With a crash like the falling apart of worlds, the engine hit the stone. It leaped, bucked, staggered like a living thing, bounced back and surged forward. Hatfield was slammed against the boiler with a force that knocked the breath from his body and set his head spinning. Another thunderous crash, a clanging and rumbling and the locomotive advanced with a roar, hurling blocks of stone in every direction. It raced ahead, its drivers rose high, fell back with a clang, raised again. Over it went to slam into the rock side wall of the tunnel and lean drunkenly, scalding steam howling from a smashed cylinder and filling the bore with a white fog.

Hatfield leaped away from the boiler head, his brain reeling. He jerked both injectors wide open, sending streams of cold water hissing into the boiler. Seizing the grate shakers, he worked them frantically, dumping the fire from the firebox. Coughing and choking in the smoke and ashes that swirled up from the scattered coals, he groped on the deck, found the mud valve lever and jerked it open. Steam and water thundering from the valve added to the uproar.

But under this triple attack, the steam

pressure in the boiler fell with magical swiftness. The whirling clouds thinned. The pandemonium lessened. Hatfield dropped to the ground and shouted to Cardigan. As the engineer and his companions came sloshing down the wet tunnel, bearing the stricken powder men, the rescuers burst through the steam clouds, shouting and cheering.

The fresh air outside soon revived the victims of the experience. Aside from an aching head and a few burns and bruises, Hatfield felt little the worse. Cardigan was in a highly nervous condition but gradually calmed. He and Hatfield ate together in a corner of the big camp dining room. The Ranger was the recipient of admiring glances from the workers. There was much low voiced talk and wagging of heads. For Cardigan had been loud in asserting that he and the others owed their lives to the Lone Wolf's resourcefulness and daring.

"Where did you learn to operate a locomotive like that?" the engineer wondered. "You handled it like an experienced hogger."

Hatfield evaded the question and managed to change the conversation. But Cardigan was due for some more wondering before the evening was over.

CHAPTER 6

Lang, the big foreman, had taken over the chore of cleaning up the mess in the tunnel and repairing the damage done, so when they had finished eating, Cardigan repaired to his office. He asked Hatfield to accompany him.

"I'd like to show you the plans of the work," he said. "Chances are you won't understand them, but perhaps I can explain them enough to make it interesting."

His face glowed with pride as he discussed his work, adding with almost boyish enthusiasm, "It's the biggest job I ever handled, and I got it through a sad accident, the death of Mr. Barnes who was given the job by Mr. Dunn, the general manager. Only," he continued, with a touch of grimness, "after what has been happening of late, I'm beginning almost to wonder if it really was an accident."

"Killed by a premature dynamite explosion, wasn't he?" Hatfield asked. "I recall Tobe Harness mentioning it."

"Not exactly, though in a way you could call it that," Cardigan replied. "Mr. Barnes always superintended in person the start of the day's drilling. The general supposition was that a stick had failed to explode when the powder was fired by the night shift before going off duty. Anyhow, when the drilling started, one of the drills hit a stick and it let go. Killed Barnes and the driller and badly injured three others. I'm wondering if that dynamite wasn't deliberately planted."

"Could have been," Hatfield admitted, "judging from what happened today."

Cardigan nodded sober agreement and began unrolling plans and laying them on a broad table. Soon he was poring over line and figures, talking volubly the while.

Hatfield watched him, simulating an interest that he did not feel. In fact, he paid but scant attention to Cardigan's lengthy and somewhat involved explanations. He was much more interested in the man himself. And as Cardigan discoursed on his work and his plans for the future, Hatfield arrived at a definite conclusion, a conclusion that was helped along by the happenings of the afternoon. It was hardly reasonable to suppose that whoever was endeavoring to delay the C & P building program, would have attempted to murder Cardigan if he was a member of the enemy group.

Finally, Cardigan rolled up the plans and placed them in a pigeonhole. There was a pleased smile on his thin face, the smile that comes from accomplishment and the knowledge of work well done. Cardigan, Hatfield definitely decided, would never be a party to schemes tending to hamper that work. His gaze roved over the office, centered on another roll of plans, a dusty roll that appeared to have rested undisturbed for quite some time in its pigeonhole.

"What's that?" he asked casually, indicating the roll.

"That? Oh, that's the plans for the bridge across Horse River," Cardigan replied, confirming what Hatfield already suspected.

"Mind if I look at them?"

"Why no, help yourself," Cardigan said.

Hatfield drew forth the roll, knocked off some of the dust and spread the sheets on the table. For long minutes he studied the tracings, his black brows drawing together. He appeared to have totally forgotten Cardigan. Finally he drew pencil and paper toward him and began to figure.

Cardigan watched him curiously. Gradually, however curiosity was supplanted by an expression of blank astonishment. Finally he crossed the room softly and stood looking over Hatfield's shoulder. The Lone Wolf, absorbed with figures and symbols, took no notice till Cardigan touched his arm. He looked up absently at the engineer.

"Hatfield," said Cardigan, "who in hell are you, anyhow?"

"Told you my name, and it happens to be my real one," the Lone Wolf replied, his mouth twitching slightly at the corners.

"You seem to know — well, considerable about these things," Cardigan remarked, gesturing to the bridge plans.

"Well," Hatfield smiled, "I've worked around a chore or two of this sort, and picked up a little knowledge concerning them."

"So I see," Cardigan returned dryly, "and while you were at it, you *picked up* a thorough grounding in the principles of higher mathematics. Why that equation there" (he stabbed at the paper with a forefinger) "the one dealing with the stresses engendered by moving water of various depths and dealing with the moment of inertia of an object subjected to such strains, that equation could only be solved by a trained mathematician. Only a highly certificated engineer could write it, much less work it out. I couldn't do it myself without recourse to half a dozen reference books, and you solved it as fast as you could scribble the symbols and figures. I ask again, who, and what the hell are you?"

Instead of answering the question, Hatfield asked one of his own.

"Cardigan, did you ever study these plans carefully and compare them with the work being done?"

"Why — why, no," Cardigan admitted, "Mr. Price handles that work. I'm not a bridge engineer, as I told you before, and he is."

"Well," Hatfield said grimly, "he's certainly not acting like a bridge engineer. He has made no attempt to follow these plans drawn by the field engineers and certified by the main office of construction. Look here, the plans call for breakwaters to be built upstream so that in high water the rapid current would be directed equally between the piers, and not against them. Where are those breakwaters? They have not been built, not even started. Does Price think they are to be built after the piers are laid? If so, he's no engineer. And over there are coffer dams that don't dam anything except 'damn' the man who built them. These plans call for fifty-foot pilings to be driven to bedrock. Not a pile has been driven. There is no solid base for any of the cribbings. No foundations for the piers."

He paused to roll a cigarette, his eyes heavy on the engineer's tragic face.

"The anchor piers," he went on, "are

based on sand, and that sand is made up of small, smooth, rounded grains. You know what that means, Cardigan. You know what happens when those grains are moistened. They slip on each other. What was a firmly packed bed when dry becomes quicksand when wet. The loose mass becomes like fluid. And what kind of support is that for a bridge pier? Let one real flood come down that river and your bridge will go out like so much straw. If those hellions who turned that creek into Horse River had built their dam a few feet higher and turned loose the impounded water, your steel work would right now be lying at the bottom of the river. And there have been thousands and thousands of dollars worth of masonry cut and laid to absolutely no purpose. And not one foot of progress has been made."

Cardigan's face was white to the lips. "Hatfield," he gasped, "are you sure you know what you're talking about? Are you sure you're not mistaken?"

"Go look for yourself," Hatfield replied.

"But — but Price," Cardigan stuttered. "Price is an engineer. I *know* he is."

A thought suddenly struck Hatfield. "Cardigan," he said, "you hired Price, I believe. Where did you get him?"

"Why — why he came here and applied

for the job," Cardigan replied. "He was introduced by Sheriff Benton and a lawyer friend of his from Sierra, Archibald Watson."

"What!"

"That's right. They both seemed to think mighty well of Price and he had excellent recommendations."

"Who recommended him?"

"The T & S W Railroad. They said he did work for them down around Laredo and proved himself thoroughly competent."

Hatfield stared at the engineer. "Cardigan," he said, "do you know anything about the T & S W?"

"Why, no."

"The T & S W," Hatfield said quietly, "is a subsidiary of the M & K. The M & K owns the T & S W lock, stock and barrel."

Cardigan's jaw dropped. His nervous mouth twitched. He raised a shaking hand and wiped his perspiring face. Hatfield suddenly felt very sorry for him.

"Cardigan," he said gently, "was Mr. Dunn here after Barnes was killed?"

"No," the engineer replied. "He had just sailed for Europe. The chief field engineer came here right after Barnes' death and talked with me. He seemed satisfied that I could carry on the work."

"I see, and was the bridge started then?"

"The approaches were being laid," Cardigan replied.

"And Price showed up after he left?"

"Yes, immediately afterward. I wired the field engineer and told him I considered Price a good man. He wired back that I could use my own discretion in the matter of assistants. He was on his way to Louisiana, where an extension is being built to the Gulf."

"Yes, that's a big project," Hatfield nodded. "Now to get back to the men who introduced Price to you. Sheriff Benton is an honest old gent who doesn't know what it is all about, or I'm a heap mistaken. I never met Watson till the other night, but I know something about him. He is the Chairman of the Committee on Corporations in the lower house of the Legislature. He directed the fight against the C & P Extension Bill. Crane Ballard owns *him,* or thinks he does. Anyhow, Watson strings along with Ballard and pulls wires for him in the Legislature. Beginning to understand?"

"Yes," Cardigan replied thickly. "Looks like I was taken in proper."

"Watson and Crane Ballard have taken in smarter men than you or I," Hatfield

110

comforted.

"Smarter than me, perhaps," Cardigan mumbled, "but I've got my doubts about them or anybody else taking in you. Hatfield, I'm going to ask again, what are you?"

"Captain of the guards here," the Lone Wolf replied.

"You have no other connections with the C & P?"

"No," Hatfield truthfully replied.

"What in blazes am I going to do?" Cardigan asked.

"You're construction engineer in charge of the project," Hatfield pointed out.

"Yes," Cardigan replied, "but as I told you, I'm no bridge engineer. If I discharge Price, who can I get to take his place in a hurry? Also, Price seems to have influential connections. I may not be able to back up my orders without an investigation by the main construction office. And that will mean more delay. Also, if Price finds I've caught on, he may do something to cause us a lot more trouble.

"And there's another angle to consider. It will be my word against his. Price can claim that he was merely obeying my orders. After all, Hatfield, I am not a famous engineer. I'm just a run-of-the-mill sort that fell into a big job by accident."

Hatfield considered. There was something to what Cardigan said. Hatfield was by now thoroughly convinced that the engineer was honest. But it was quite obvious that he was not a strong character, that he was not sure of himself outside of the work he was doing. Cardigan had fallen into the position he now occupied after the unexpected death of Barnes, the man chosen by General Manager Dunn to forward the project. The travelling engineer, a very busy man with much on his hands, had investigated Cardigan's work on the cut and the tunnel and had decided that he was competent and capable of carrying on. At that time, the bridge with its totally different problems was not yet under way. The traveling engineer had doubtless assumed that Cardigan would also be able to handle that in a satisfactory manner. He had slipped a mite in not questioning Cardigan's ability more thoroughly. He had taken a little too much for granted. Cardigan, knowing his own limitations, had hired a man who was a specialist in bridge building: Sime Price. And Price was actually in the pay of M & K and furthering that road's end, Hatfield was sure.

But there was no real proof that Price was Crane Ballard's man. The fact that he had once worked for the T & S W did not alone constitute conclusive proof. Captains of industry and finance don't usually confide their sometimes questionable schemes to comparatively obscure underlings. If Price maintained vigorously he was but carrying out Cardigan's orders, Cardigan might be hard put to clear himself. Price was aggressive, Cardigan was not. Hatfield suspected that Price would be able to make out a good case for himself. Cardigan was liable to get flustered and damn himself with inconclusive statements.

And at the moment, Hatfield had no authority with which to back up Cardigan. With General Manager Dunn somewhere at sea, it was problematical when there would be a chance of his getting it.

And meanwhile the whole project was being slowed down, with the ever deadly danger of a bad flood wreaking well nigh irreparable destruction.

"Looks like I'm sort of getting off trail from Ranger work," he mused, "but I'm playing a strong hunch that the two will tie up together. This railroad business is my only real hope that the hellions will tip their hand."

Cardigan was fingering his nervous lips.

He glanced appealingly at the Lone Wolf.

"Hatfield," he repeated, "what am I going to do?"

"We'll sleep on it," Hatfield replied. "Maybe something will work out tomorrow. Incidentally, I want you to do something for me."

"Anything I can," the engineer assured him.

"I want you," Hatfield said slowly, "to eat dinner in Ace Turner's Red Cow tomorrow evening. Have a couple of drinks first and then something to eat. Then here is what you do —"

As Cardigan listened to Hatfield's instructions, a bewildered look overspread his face. He shook his head, stared at the Ranger.

"It sure doesn't make sense to me," he said, "but if you tell me to, I'll do it."

Hatfield visited the telegraph office the following morning, and again in the afternoon with barren results. There was no message from Jaggers Dunn.

Toward evening, one of the men assigned to guard the trestle and the bridge showed up.

"My relief got there and took over," he told Hatfield. "Didn't I say Price would raise hell? He sure did, but we told him we had our orders and were going to stay on the job. He said he'd see Cardigan about that and figured to tell you off proper when you showed at the bridge. Hope I'll be there to see it."

"Chances are you will," Hatfield replied briefly. "I'm riding out there tomorrow or next day."

The guard departed, grinning expectantly.

Later, as he promised Hatfield he would do, Lane Cardigan sat down in the Red Cow, ordered several drinks and consumed them. Then he ate a hearty meal. After finishing his dinner, he beckoned the waiter who served him. The waiter laboriously totalled up his bill and gave it to him. Cardigan reached into his pocket. A blank expression crossed his face.

"By George!" he exclaimed, "seems I left my wallet at the camp. Call Mr. Turner, please."

The waiter summoned Ace Turner who strolled over to the table. Cardigan explained his predicament to him.

"It's perfectly all right, Mr. Cardigan," Turner assured the engineer. "In fact, you might as well have this on me."

"No, no, I couldn't do that," Cardigan protested. "After all, business is business."

"But if it wasn't for you fellers, I wouldn't have any business," Turner replied genially.

"Give me that check."

He leaned over, drew a pencil from his pocket and wrote a single word across the bottom of the slip.

"That takes care of it, John," he told the waiter. "And bring Mr. Cardigan a night-cap."

With a nod, he returned to the bar. The waiter shambled off to procure the drink, leaving the okayed check on the table. Cardigan absently laid his hat over it. When he arose from the table, he picked up his hat and check together. The waiter, after a perfunctory search, grumbled something under his breath and forgot all about the matter.

A little later, in Cardigan's office, Jim Hatfield gazed at the slip of paper with glowing eyes. Beneath the waiter's crabbed figures, in a cold, flowing hand, was the single word — *"Roof!"*

CHAPTER 7

That night, Hatfield was sitting by the open window of the bunkhouse smoking and thinking deeply. A poker game was in progress in one corner of the bunkhouse, where the men off duty wrangled over their cards. The night was very still. Overhead the glowing stars seemed to brush the hilltops. The crags stood tall and black against the velvety sky. A faint wind soughed out of the east.

On the wings of the wind, there suddenly came a sound, a deep and hollow boom. Hatfield started. The poker players looked up questioningly.

"What in blazes was that?" one wondered. "Sounded like dynamite. But they ain't doin' any blastin' at the tunnel."

Hatfield leaned out the window listening intently. The sound was not repeated.

"It wasn't overly far off," he muttered. He stood up abruptly.

"I'm going to take a little ride," he told the guards. "You fellers stick around. Might want you later."

With wondering glances following his tall form, he strode from the bunkhouse and hurried to the nearby stable. As he got the rig on Goldy, an eastbound material train of empties clattered past.

"Maybe I should have flagged that rattler," he grunted, "but somehow I feel better on a horse. And they won't make much better time than Goldy will, at that."

He swung into the saddle, settled his feet in the stirrups.

"Sift sand, jughead," he told the sorrel,

"I've got a mighty strong hunch that some hell-raising has been under way. Trail!"

The golden horse shot forward, his irons drumming the hard surface of the trail. The twin ribbons of steel flowed past. Trees rushed toward them and dwindled away behind. Overhead the stars burned in the Texas sky. Below was a world of shadows dimly outlined in the glint of starlight. The cliffs rode black and sheer with the wind whispering softly over their serried battlements. The beat of Goldy's hoofs rang loud in the silence. Hatfield eyed the trail ahead, his brows drawn together. From force of long habit, he rode alert and watchful.

But nothing broke the peace of the quiet night as the flying horse covered mile after mile. Then, Hatfield slowly became conscious of a confused murmur ahead. A moment later he sighted the sullen red lights of the rear markers of the material train. The long string of cars stood motionless. He flashed by the flagman standing far back with his red and white lanterns.

"Thought so," Hatfield muttered. "It's that infernal trestle. Something's happened, all right. The whole camp is roused up."

He had identified the confused murmur as the shouts and excited talk of a large number of men. He whisked past the hissing locomotive and a scene of wild confusion confronted him. The river bank was black with men who ran about aimlessly, shouting and gesticulating. Numerous flares had been lighted and their forms were outlined in the ruddy glare.

Outlined too, was the trestle across the river. The west end sagged drunkenly and seemed on the verge of plunging into the water.

As Hatfield unforked, Maloney, the big mason, came running up, a rifle in his hand.

"The owlhoots tried to blow the west trestle approach wth dynamite," he told Hatfield. "They would have done it too, if I hadn't been perched up in the superstructure with me gun. I been suspicious of what might happen and sort of kept an eye on things. Was just gettin' ready to knock off and grab a wee bit of sleep when I saw something moving on the approach and a little light. I slid over that way and saw two men doin' somethin' atop the stone work. I let out a beller and one of 'em took a shot at me. I cut loose with my Winchester, emptyin' the magazine. I got one of those jiggers, I'm pretty sure. I heard a yell and then a splash. Reckon he went into the river. A minute all hell busted loose and I nearly went into the river. Thought the trestle was goin' in, too, but it didn't. Figure they didn't have time to plant the sticks properly. Just blew off part of the copin' and let the span sag."

"Good man!" Hatfield said briefly. "Wait here, Maloney." He turned to the conductor of the material train, who was listening to what Maloney said.

"Back up your train to the camp," Hatfield told him. "Try and find Mr. Cardigan. Tell him I sent you. Tell him to rush every available man here with jacks, plenty of them, and timbers and at least two more derricks. We've got to raise that trestle span and straighten it out before it drops in the river. It won't take much more pounding from the water. The supporting pier is out of line. Take it easy on the way and keep red fuses burning on the rear end. You might meet something coming this way, although it's doubtful at this time of night. Move!"

The conductor "moved" as the last word blared at him. He shouted to the engineer, went scrambling up the grabirons to the top of the head car and started running over the car tops to the rear. The engineer blew three short blasts, threw his locomotive into reverse and cracked the throttle. With a jangling of couplers and grinding of tires the material train rumbled back to the camp.

Hatfield turned to Maloney. "Where are my guards?" he asked. "Bill Purdy and Bert King were on duty here."

"That's what I've been wonderin' about," replied Maloney. "I ain't seen hide or hair of either one of 'em. The boys on the east end of the trestle are okay. I talked with 'em a minute ago."

"Come on," Hatfield ordered tersely. "Scatter out and comb the brush around the trestle approach. They couldn't have blown that approach without getting them out of the way first."

Not far from the tracks and only a few yards west of the approach they found Purdy. His head had been crushed by a heavy blow. A long knife was driven between his shoulder blades.

Hatfield's face was bleak as the granite of the hills, his eyes coldly gray as he gazed at the dead man. He had liked Bill Purdy, a genial, cheerful person, quite a contrast to the man who worked as his partner. King was lean and sunken and uncommunicative, a cowhand from the southwest.

"Bert sure don't talk," Hatfield recalled Purdy saying, "but he sure don't miss no bets, either. A good man. I like to work with him. Feel things are under control when Bert is keepin' an eye on 'em."

It seemed, however, that Purdy had over-estimated King's abilities.

"Look around for what's left of King," Hatfield told the searchers.

The men scattered out, poking and peering through the brush. A moment later one shouted, "Here's his horse, Purdy's too. Both of 'em tied here in the brush."

Both horses were saddled and bridled. King's rifle was in the boot. But there was no sign of the taciturn cowhand. After a prolonged search that extended over a wide area without results, Hatfield called the men in.

Soon afterward, the material train returned with everything necessary for the repair of the trestle. With the train was a badly worried Cardigan.

"My God! will it ever end!" he said. "Two more men dead! Hatfield, this is awful."

Hatfield nodded sober agreement. "But anyhow they didn't pull what they hoped to, thanks to Maloney," he observed. "Straightening out that trestle and anchoring it again isn't much of a chore. The foreman can handle it after you get them started. And Price should be back from town when the regular day's work begins."

The stars were paling from gold to silver and the smell of dawn was in the air. A second material train arrived with more timbers, tools and men. These piled off in the graying light and hurried to the scene of operations.

The sun was well up before Hatfield and Cardigan found a few minutes to spare. Then they repaired to the bunkhouse to examine the body of the slain guard. For some minutes, Hatfield studied the dead man, his brows drawing together. Cardigan watched him expectantly.

"Find out anything?" the engineer asked at length.

"Yes," Hatfield said, "that Purdy was struck down from the front by a man facing him. Notice where the blow landed, just above the left temple and to the front. I'd say he'd turned his head slightly when he was hit."

"And what does that mean?" asked the puzzled Cardigan.

"That's what I hope to find out," Hatfield replied slowly, and Cardigan noticed that his eyes had subtly changed color. They were no longer the sunny green of a summer sea, but the cold gray of that same sea storm-tossed under a cloudy sky.

"Come on," Hatfield said abruptly, "let's

take a walk."

He led the way to the spot where the body of Purdy was discovered.

"Stay back," he warned the engineer and began intently studying the ground.

The soil was soft at that point, and boot prints were plainly discernible. Hatfield finally pointed to the ground and motioned Cardigan to come closer.

"See them?" he asked. "Among the prints left by the workers' hob-nailed soles. Two sets of high-heeled boot tracks. You'll notice the toes are pointing toward each other. Two men stood here talking — two men wearing cowhand boots. Stood for some time. You can see how the prints shifted slightly. Right here is where Purdy was killed, by a man talking with him, a man I'd say he had no reason to fear. Otherwise the prints left by the killer would have come up behind him and he would have been struck down unawares. He was struck down unawares as it was. Doubtless when he turned his head to look at something the other pointed out. Then the man who struck him made doubly sure by driving that knife into his heart."

"But what in blazes?" demanded the bewildered engineer. "Who would do such a thing, and why?"

"The last question is easily answered,"

Hatfield replied. "So the killer would have all the time he needed to plant the dynamite charge. You can't plant that amount of dynamite properly in a hurry. Takes time. The killer wanted to make sure he would be able to work uninterrupted."

"And you think they did for King, the other guard, the same way and threw his body in the river?" Cardigan asked.

"That remains to be found out," Hatfield replied. "Anyhow, the man who killed Purdy had to be sure Purdy wouldn't be able to talk. He couldn't count on just the blow on the head."

Cardigan swore explosively and shook his fist to the north. Hatfield apparently took no notice of the gesture. He was staring southwest toward where the mountains of the lower Big Bend shouldered against the sky.

"Cardigan," he said suddenly, "I seem to recollect Tobe Harness saying that Bert King was a cowhand on a ranch down to the southwest of here before he drifted up in this direction and took a job with the guards."

"That's right," replied Cardigan.

"Do you by any chance remember the name of the outfit he said he worked for?" Hatfield asked.

"Yes, I do," Cardigan replied. "The name struck me as unusual and rather amusing. It was *I Owe You*."

"Named for the brand mark, I O U," Hatfield translated with a smile. "I've heard of it. It's a big spread owned by a gent named I. O. Utley. It's the sort of a holding that has a considerable turnover of hands. Men get tired of that desolate region and drift on to more interesting sections. How did you come to hire King? Somebody recommend him?"

"Yes," Cardigan replied, looking queerly at the Ranger. "Yes, he was recommended by Arch Watson, the lawyer."

"What!" Hatfield exploded.

"That's right," Cardigan nodded. "I understand Watson owns property down around where that ranch is located. He knew King there, so when King wanted a job with the guards — you know we screened them rather carefully, or tried to — he went to Watson and asked him to put in a word for him. Watson did so, and I hired King."

For a moment Hatfield was silent, digesting this piece of news. Then he said, "Come on, I want to take a look at the ground where they found those two horses tied."

When they reached the spot, easily located by the marks left by the stamping horses, Hatfield went over the ground with the greatest care, following a constantly widening circle with the spot as the center. Suddenly he uttered an exclamation.

"Here's where another horse was tied," he told Cardigan. "You can see where he stood for a considerable time, and the bark is chafed on that limb beside you. And here are his tracks going away from here, heading south to the trail. The horse used by the killer to make his get-away, I'd say."

"Makes sense," Cardigan admitted. "Looks like one or two men took care of the chore."

"One expert powder man and a helper could handle it without any trouble," Hatfield explained. "Really one man was all they needed. A man with cold nerve and plenty of savvy. But maybe he did not have quite enough savvy, although he did pretty well put it over on us, in the beginning. Maybe he slipped just a mite."

Cardigan glanced questioningly at the Ranger, but Hatfield only said, "Let's get back to the camp. You can stand some shut-eye."

"And you?" Cardigan asked.

"Me? I figure to take a little ride," Hatfield said.

The "little ride" Hatfield took kept him in the saddle all that day. He skirted the towering Bullis Gap Mountains, rode through the pass between the Santiagos and the Del Nortes and rounded the southwesterly tip of the Cienagas. Just as the sun was setting, he rode up to a big white ranchhouse built in a grove. A big old man, Irving Owen Utley, owner of the I O U, sat on the front porch in a comfortably tilted-back chair, his high boot heels hooked over a rung.

"Light off and cool your saddle, cowboy," he shouted hospitably. "Be chuck on the table in half an hour. Come up and set. I'll have a wrangler take care of your critter."

Hatfield accepted the invitation, after first "introducing" the wrangler to Goldy.

"Otherwise you couldn't touch him," he explained. "Mr. Utley, isn't it?" he addressed his host.

"That's right," said the ranch owner. Hatfield supplied his own name and they shook hands.

"Chuck line ridin'?" asked Utley.

"Sort of," Hatfield admitted. "Had a little business to attend to down in this section and figured maybe I'd ought to drop in on you while I was here. 'Fraid I've got some bad news for you about a feller who used to work for you. Understand you thought pretty well of him. Seems to have got himself cashed in."

"That so?" Utley replied with interest. "Must have been somebody who rode for me quite a spell back. My hands don't often quit me. Most of 'em been with me for years. What was the feller's name?"

"King," Hatfield replied — "Bert King."

Utley knit his brows. "Can't seem to recall the name," he said at length. "What did the feller look like?"

Hatfield supplied a description of the missing cowhand. Utley shook his head.

"Somebody must have slipped up or you got the spread name wrong," he said. "Don't remember ever havin' anybody like that workin' for me. Who told you the feller had been one of my hands?"

"A lawyer fellow," Hatfield replied, "Archibald Watson, who represents the county in the Legislature. He 'lowed you told him you thought mighty well of King."

A scowl darkened Utley's face. "Now I know darn well you got the wrong slant," he growled. "If that damn shyster come onto my place I'd take a shotgun to him."

"You don't think well of Watson?" Hatfield asked in surprised tones.

"You're damn right I don't," replied Utley. "He's one of those damned squirmy sidewinders who always manages to pull his skullduggery just inside the law, but it's skullduggery just the same. Mean as a Gila monster, and just as deadly. I knew him back in the days when he was runnin' guns across the River to troublemakers below the Line and smugglin' in stuff like that damned pizen marihuana. That was before he got to be a lawyer and hoodwinked folks into votin' for him. Sets up to be a gentleman, now, but he sure didn't used to be. Dangerous, though. Plumb deadly with a gun, and don't let his fat fool you. That's all on the outside. Under it he's hard as iron, and there sure ain't no fat above his eyes. Smart as a treeful of owls. I'm damn glad that feller King never rode for me, if Watson stands up for him. Critters of the same brand have a habit of herdin' together. Figure if he'd rode for me, I'd be short cows."

Hatfield enjoyed a good dinner and slept at the ranchhouse. After an early breakfast he said goodbye to the hospitable Utley and rode off. After he had disappeared around a bend in the trail, Utley remarked contemplatively to his range boss, "Hank, I wouldn't want to be Hank, and I sure wouldn't want him on my trail. No boots?" snorted the range boss.

"Who the hell *would* want to be in a dead man's in that King jigger's boots."

"Got a hunch he ain't dead," said Utley. "Chances are he'd be better off if he was and had it over with. Feller didn't say he was dead. Just said he seemed to have got himself cashed in. That big feller's on his trail, sir-eee!"

Jim Hatfield wore a satisfied expression as he rode steadily north by east at a fast pace. "It was a straight hunch, horse," he told Goldy. "Now I've got a prime notion who is the big he-wolf of the pack. A lot of things that have been puzzling me are cleared up. But why in hell couldn't it have been King that Maloney shot off the trestle approach instead of the other one!"

When Hatfield got back to the camp, Cardigan welcomed him with evident relief.

"The ways things have been going around here, I was getting worried that something might have happened to you," he said. "No, nothing else has gone wrong since you left."

"But I'm afraid things are liable to happen, things we won't like," Hatfield returned, with a glance at the lowering sky.

"You rode away for some particular reason?" Cardigan asked.

Hatfield nodded. "Yes, I did," he replied. "And I learned plenty."

Cardigan looked expectant. Hatfield rolled and lighted a cigarette before speaking.

"Yes, I learned plenty," he repeated, "among other things who it was killed Bill Purdy."

"You did!" exclaimed the engineer. "Who was it?"

"Bert King," Hatfield said.

Cardigan looked astonished. "But — but, King was working with Purdy and we found his horse," he stuttered.

"We found the horse he intended us to find," Hatfield replied quietly. "King rode off on that other horse we found tied a little farther on. That's where King slipped. He left that horse tied a mite too close. As I told you, Purdy was killed by a man he had no reason to fear, a man wearing cowboy boots. Could have been none other than King. None of the construction workers wear cowboy boots. And," he added impressively, "Arch Watson slipped and slipped bad when he eased King into the guard force. I learned that King never worked for the spread, the I O U that Watson said he worked for. Old Irv Utley has no use for Watson and handed me a bit of interesting information relative to Watson's former activities."

"Good God!" exclaimed Cardigan. "What shall we do? Confront Watson with what you learned, or have him thrown in jail?"

Hatfield smiled and shook his head. "We have absolutely nothing on Watson that would hold up in court," he replied. "He could disavow the whole thing, say he made a mistake about King, that King lied to him and took him in, that he only figured to do a constituent a favor, common enough practice with politicians. They recommend people they know little or nothing about. Anything to get the votes. That would provide an excuse for Watson it would be hard to question. No, we can only wait till a few more loose ends are tied up."

CHAPTER 8

One of the reasons for Jim Hatfield's outstanding success as a Ranger was his almost uncanny ability to spot the weak link in a shady organization. In the present instance, Hatfield felt that Bert King was the weak link in an otherwise very strong chain. He determined to concentrate on King. A trip to the telegraph office brought no word from Jaggers Dunn, and Hatfield still hesitated to make a drastic move without authority. The thing might easily backfire unpleasantly. Sheriff Benton, he knew, was an associate of Arch Watson's and held the legislator in high esteem. Benton was a "party" man and felt that Watson was an asset to the party. This alone was enough, to strongly influence the honest but rather stupid old peace officer in Watson's favor. Hatfield felt sure that if a showdown came, Benton would side with Watson and without revealing his Ranger connections, which he did not want to do at the moment, he couldn't buck Benton's authority as a peace officer. So he decided that King was his best bet. The question was, how to get a line on King.

After due consideration, he approached Cardigan.

"As I said before," he told the engineer, "we have absolutely nothing on anybody except King. I can hang a murder charge on King and make it stick, and in this section that means the rope sure as hell. Corral King and there's a good chance that he'll talk to save his own neck. Very seldom do you find anything like honor or loyalty in an owlhoot organization. Each member primarily serves his own best interests. They'll stick together so long as it is to their advantage as individuals to do so. But self-interest is the real motivation of each. Let his own interests be jeopardized, and the average law breaker will turn on his fellows like a sidewinder biting himself when a road-runner teases him till he goes loco."

Cardigan nodded sober agreement. Hatfield sat silent for some moments, smoking thoughtfully.

"Do you happen to know if King had any close associates among the guards or the other workers?" he asked suddenly.

Cardigan shook his head. "Not that I know of," he replied. "In fact I recall Tobe Harness mentioning that he sure seemed to be the lone wolf type. Kept very much to himself. Stop, though, I happen to remember something that might be of significance. The day we hired King we hired another man. They showed up together, although they showed no indication of being acquainted. I remember these things because I made a point of questioning the guards myself — thought it was a good idea because of the importance of their work. We hired Craig Ord the same day we hired King. And Ord is from the southwest section, too, or so he said. He told a very straight story and gave outfits he worked for as references. Harness said he knew one of those outfits and that it had an excellent reputation. I told Harness to look it up about Ord, and I presume he did, seeing as he okayed the hiring a little later. And here's something else that might be important. Ord got very friendly with Bill Purdy. In fact, Ord asked to be transferred to the night shift so that he and Purdy could ride together and go to town together in the daytime. They always did on their days off."

"I think it's worth looking into," Hatfield admitted. "When is Ord's next day off?"

"Tomorrow," he said.

Shortly after midnight, when the other occupants were sound asleep, Hatfield slipped out of the bunkhouse and repaired to the stable. He got the rig on Goldy and led him from the stable without arousing the stablekeeper. He mounted the sorrel and sent him north by slightly west. In his saddle pouches he had a few simple and compact cooking utensils and some staple provisions, for he did not know how protracted his stay in the hills might be.

The hours passed slowly. Then he saw nothing but the lonely stars and heard nothing but the whisper of the wind through the leaves, the mournful plaint of an owl and occasionally the haunting, beautiful call of a hunting wolf. He reasoned that if Ord had a definite reason for riding into the hills, perhaps to carry provisions to the occupant of some hole-up, he would doubtless repeat the trip on this, his day off.

The sun rose in glory, banishing the shadows and flooding the land with a tremulous golden glow. Hatfield got the rig on Goldy and sat gazing southward.

An hour passed and nothing happened. Then suddenly the Ranger stiffened to attention.

To the south he had sighted movement. At first he thought it might be a wandering cow, but he quickly decided that the object was moving too swiftly for a beef critter. It grew larger as he watched. Details resolved. Soon he realized that it was a lone horseman riding south at a good pace.

As the rider drew nearer, Hatfield saw that if he held to his present course he would pass within a few hundred yards of the ridge. Intent with interest he watched the man's approach. He was mounted on a big blue moros that gave indications of speed and endurance. Nearer and nearer he came without swerving or slackening speed. Now he was opposite Hatfield, a little more than a hundred yards distant. The Ranger leaned forward, rigid with excitement, his eyes narrowing.

For in the rangy figure, the lean, bronzed

face and the light colored hair of the horseman, he recognized Craig Ord.

Straight for the canyon Ord rode, glancing neither to right nor left. He entered the gorge and Hatfield watched horse and rider grow small with distance and vanish around a bend.

Hatfield mounted Goldy and sent the sorrel scudding down the slope and across the level ground to the canyon mouth. A hundred yards from the towering portals he slowed down and proceeded with caution. Nothing happened, however, and the sun rays showed no living thing amid the jumble of boulders and the straggle of brush that cluttered the canyon. Hatfield sent Goldy forward and soon was riding in the shadow of the towering wall.

Soon Hatfield realized he was following a fairly well defined trail, a trail that gave indications of recent use. His interest quickened and he increased the sorrel's pace a little. He saw nothing of Ord, however, but as the guard had nearly a mile's start, this was not strange.

The floor of the canyon began to rise gently. Another ten minutes and he sighted his quarry just topping the crest of the rise and perhaps five hundred yards distant. It seemed to Hatfield that his pose was one of expectancy, his head turning from side to side as if in search of something. However, he did not look back. Hatfield eased Goldy into the deeper shadow until Ord had vanished over the ridge crest. Then he quickened the sorrel's pace appreciably, confident that the intervening ridge would throw back the sound of his irons on the stones. As he neared the crest he slowed once more, hugging the beetling cliffs and rode with every sense at hair-trigger alertness.

He heard nothing, saw nothing. Slowly, carefully, he paced the sorrel ahead, his right hand close to his gun.

After a quarter of a mile of tedious going, the gloom deepening, Hatfield muttered under his breath as the cleft, curving to parallel the main canyon, began to widen. His straining ears could hear no click of irons on the stone to denote he was closing in on Ord. Once he thought he heard a sound ahead and paused to listen. But it was not repeated and he rode on.

Suddenly he sniffed sharply. To his nostrils had come a faint but pungent tang of wood smoke. He peered ahead but still could see nothing except the thickening growth. Occasional trees were starting up from the gorge floor. Hatfield paced slowly past one that threw its spreading branches low across the trail.

From above, sounded a stealthy rustling. Hatfield flung up his head an instant too late. A rope swished down from the leafy screen, a loop settled over his shoulders and was instantly jerked tight. As Goldy gave a startled plunge, Hatfield was swept from the saddle and struck the ground wth terrific force. Half stunned, before he could make a move, men leaped from the brush on either side and pinned him to the ground. His guns were jerked from their holsters, his hands tied. Then, still dizzy and reeling, he was hauled to his feet.

"All right," growled one of his captors, "straight ahead and don't try anything if you want to stay healthy. Bring the horse along, Pete."

But Goldy had other notions. Gleaming teeth slashed at the hand reaching for his bit iron. As the man jumped back with a curse, the sorrel whirled and streaked it back down the trail.

"Let him go," ordered the speaker. "We'll catch him tomorrow."

A man came sliding down the trunk of the tree from where he had made the throw that was the Ranger's undoing.

"Ain't twirled a loop for a long time, but

reckon I ain't forgot how," he remarked with an evil chuckle.

With a gun muzzle prodding his back, Hatfield stumbled forward. His head was still ringing from the fall but his mind was clearing and his strength was coming back. He was seething with rage directed at himself.

"An old trick and I fell for it," he muttered under his breath. "The hellion must have known all the time I was trailing him and led me right into a trap."

A few minutes of walking and Hatfield saw an ancient cabin strongly built of logs and almost hidden by thick and tall chaparral. It was roofed with split poles. From the stick and mud chimney rose a trickle of smoke. Nearby was a lean-to under which were tethered several horses. Among them, Hatfield recognized Craig Ord's blue moros. He gritted his teeth with anger as his captors shoved him toward the cabin door.

With the gun muzzle still prodding him, he entered, his captors crowding around him. He was pushed into a chair. His ankles were securely lashed to the stout chair legs. His captors stepped back.

The first thing Hatfield's eyes rested on was Craig Ord seated opposite him and similarly trussed up.

CHAPTER 9

Ord grinned rather wanly as he met the Ranger's astonished gaze. He shook his head in sympathy.

Hatfield's glance shifted from Ord's pale and blood-streaked face and took in the other occupants of the room. Beside his three captors, there were two others. One was standing beside a glowing stove and grinning maliciously. The other was seated at a table littered with dirty dishes. His features were hidden by a black mask.

His gaze steady on the mask, Hatfield spoke, in quiet, level tones.

"All right, King," he said. "You might as well take that rag off your face. I know you."

The masked man nodded. "Yes," he replied, "reckon I might as well. What you know or don't know doesn't matter much any more."

For a long minute, King regarded the Ranger in silence.

"So," he said at length, "slipped up a mite, it'd seem. I've a notion you are sort of overestimated — ain't nearly so smart as most folks think or you wouldn't have fallen for it. I figured that, sooner or later, you'd start keeping tabs on Ord, especially after he began nosing around the canyon. Figured

I'd get the chance to bag both of you, which I did. It might interest you, Ord, to know that the breed who told you he'd seen me in the canyon was — well, an *amigo* of mine. I figured you couldn't resist the chance to get a line on me. Didn't think you'd go to the sheriff or Hatfield with the yarn. 'Lowed you'd want to kill me yourself. And figured Hatfield would be keepin' an eye open and wonder what the hell you were up to."

He paused, smiling thinly, and rolled a cigarette. It was Craig Ord's turn to grit his teeth in futile rage.

"I could have bagged you the first time you came snoopin' up here and found nobody," King pursued, "but I wanted Hatfield, too. And now I've got you both."

He leaned forward, his features suddenly convulsed with hatred, his pale eyes glittering insanely.

"I've got good reason to hate everything your kind of jigger stands for, Hatfield," he told the Ranger. "Your sort robbed me of some of the best years of my life. Kind of nice to get even."

He sank back in his chair, panting with the wrath that consumed him. Jim Hatfield abruptly realized that he had to deal with a madman and an utterly snake-blooded one at that. He continued to rest his steady gaze on King's face, and say nothing.

"Thought you'd like to know how it was done," King resumed, his voice quiet again, his features composed. "Well, you know now, but knowing won't do you much good. All right, boys, rig 'em up."

Two of the men approached Hatfield. Working deftly and swiftly, they slipped a noose over the Ranger's head and around his throat. The noose was so tight it constricted his breathing and allowed but scant movement. Hatfield felt the hard protuberance of a hangman's knot under his left ear. Then while one held the muzzle of a gun against the back of his head, the other man cut the ropes that bound Hatfield's wrists and jerked his arms high above his head. Around his wrists he slipped a second noose and drew it tight. Then he stepped back, grinning evilly. The other two men had performed a like office for Craig Ord.

"Don't try to lower your arms," King warned Hatfield. "Look up and you'll see why."

Hatfield glanced up, uncomprehending at first. Then his eyes narrowed and his jaw set hard as he sat and understood the simple but viciously ingenious contrivance above his head.

Spanning the room of the cabin from eave

to eave under the low peaked roof were three heavy beams. And bolted to the center beam so that they moved freely on a swivel in a vertical angle were two timbers. The free end of one was directly over his head, that of the other over Ord's. To these ends were affixed the hangman's ropes.

The other ends of the timbers were weighted with heavy stones. It seemed strange at first that the timbers should remain level, with their ends weighted down by the ponderous rocks. Then Hatfield saw that the unweighted ends were held fast by rawhide straps passing over them. These straps were bolted to the cross beams at one end. The other end of each was held fast by a simple trip mechanism of the ratchet and pawl type. To these trips were fastened the rope which noosed the wrists of the captives.

Hatfield saw at a glance that if he lowered his arms the tightened line would instantly spring the trip and release the unweighted end of the timber. Once released, the weight on the far end would cause it to spring upward with great force, tightening the hangman's rope and very effectively hanging the man around whose neck was the noose. With the heavy knot under his left ear, his neck would undoubtedly be broken instantly when he was jerked upward.

"Get the notion?" King asked pleasantly. "The game is to see which one will get tired first and hang the other. When your arms get to aching too much, Hatfield, just haul 'em down and watch Ord do a dance on nothing."

Again his eyes blazed insanely and on his face was an expression of awful gloating. He stood up and shifted his gun belts a trifle.

"We got a little chore to do," he said, "but we'll be back later to see who got hung first. We'll leave your body, Hatfield, here in the cabin. Ord's we'll throw in the river. Then if a search party happens to stumble on this shack, they'll figure Ord did for you, Hatfield, and then trailed his twine. Hawkins, leave Hatfield's guns alone. Leave them on the table. I know they're good irons, but you're not packin' 'em. Guns like those are out of ordinary and somebody might recognize 'em. All right, let's go."

The man who had picked up Hatfield's big Colts and was eyeing them avariciously slammed them back onto the table with a growl and slouched out after the others. The door banged shut. A moment later hoofbeats clicked away down the gorge.

In the cabin, Hatfield studied the devilish

contrivance above his head with an intensity that amounted to mental agony. He knew that if there was anything to do, it must be done swiftly. Already his arms were aching intolerably. He glanced at Ord. The guard's face was beaded with sweat. His lips were bloodless and he was trembling in every muscle.

"I can't stand this long," he panted. "Listen, feller, one of us has got to go. I'm not much good to anybody. Drop your arms and get it over with. That way you'll stay alive to even things up with those sidewinders."

"Shut up," Hatfield told him. "You're plumb white, but we'll either both come through or we'll go out together. Keep quiet, now, and let me do a mite of figuring."

Gritting his teeth against the pain in his numbing arms, he continued to study the mechanism above his head.

"Ord," he exclaimed suddenly, "I believe we've got a chance. There's something those varmints didn't figure on. My arms and my fingers are a heap sight longer than the average. I believe I can get my fingers around this infernal hangman's rope. If I can do that, you let your arms drop and release the trip. With a good grip on the hanging rope,

I'll be jerked up by my arms instead of my neck. Then you can wiggle your wrists loose, smash your chair and come over and cut me down. It may not work, but it's a chance, anyhow."

"Damn it, you couldn't never do it," gasped Ord. "The jerk would pull your fingers loose from the rope and you'd be hanged sure as shootin'. I can't let you take the chance."

"Don't bother your head about the chance I'm taking," Hatfield told him grimly. "You'll be taking the same chance. If my hands are jerked loose, my arms will drop and spring your trip, too. Then you'll get your taste of hanging. Don't you see how they have it figured out? No matter who gives out first, we'll hang each other. Hold on a minute longer. Here we go!"

With the utmost care he moved his bound wrists sideways, watching the cord to see that no strain was put upon it. As he predicted, his extraordinarily long hands and fingers enabled him to get a hold a couple of feet above his head on the rope that noosed his neck. With both hands partially around the rope, he gripped it with every ounce of his great strength.

"Now!" he gasped. "Let's go!"

Sobbing a curse, Ord jerked his arms

down sharply. There was a grinding creak as the trip snapped free. The end of the timber swung upward with terrific force. Hatfield was jerked off the floor, chair and all. One hand was torn loose by the strain, but the other retained a vise-like grip on the rope and he hung dangling.

"Hurry, feller, hurry," he gasped. "Can't take much of this."

Ord struggled madly to free his wrists. The slipknot of the noose was stubbornly tight and resisted his efforts. Moans and curses dripped from his lips. Sweat streamed down his face. At last, with a mighty jerk he loosened the noose and freed first one hand and then the other. He tried to stand up and sprawled on the floor. Madly he thrashed about, hammering the chair against the floor boards with a terrific pounding that quickly smashed it to matchwood. He scrambled to his feet, lurched to where Hatfield dangled and jerked the noose from around his neck. A knife lay amid the litter of dirty dishes on the nearby table. Ord seized it and slashed Hatfield's wrists free.

Hatfield let go his hold and thudded to the floor, breathing in great gasps. Ord cut the cords that bound his ankles to the chair legs and sank to the floor himself, half unconscious from pain and fatigue.

Hatfield recovered quickly. He staggered erect and instinctively reached for his guns lying on the table. With a feeling of intense satisfaction he holstered them. Then he turned his attention to Ord who was sitting up pale and trembling but with his strength coming back.

On the stove, the grates of which still glowed redly, was a big coffee pot. It turned out to be half full of hot coffee. Hatfield rooted out a clean tin cup, filled it and held it to Ord's lips. The guard drank the scalding liquid in gulps. He wiped his lips, smiled wanly.

"I'm all right now," he said and got slowly to his feet.

Hatfield poured himself a cup of coffee and drank thirstily. Ord was glancing about the room. Suddenly he made a dive for a belt hanging on a peg driven into the wall.

"My gun!" he exclaimed happily as he buckled it on. "They left it, too. Now we're ready for the snakes when they come back."

"You're darn right, we are," Hatfield agreed, grimly, pouring more coffee. "It's the showdown, feller. Chances are it'll be a shooting. I don't think King will give up. He's a madman if there ever was one — plumb loco. Lucky for us he is, though. If he was an ordinary hellion he would have just plugged us and got it over with, but the notion of torturing us first appealed to his crazy mind. From what he said, I've a notion he spent a good many years in prison. Sort of turned his head, I reckon, and set him plumb on the prod against all law officers and decent citizens."

Ord gazed curiously at the hanging mechanism. "Think he figured that thing out and built it?" he asked.

Hatfield shook his head. "Don't think so," he replied. "This shack is old, a couple of hundred years at least, I'd say. And that thing up there is old, too. You'll notice those ratchet wheels aren't made of iron. They were carved out of hardwood. Like as not that contrivance was set up years and years ago, maybe by the old Spaniards, and used to make fellers tell where they had gold or other treasure hidden. Those old hellions were good at that sort of thing. Chances are King stumbled onto this cabin and decided to make it his hide-out. It's a good one, all right. Nobody ever has occasion to come up here, and if anybody ever did, and stumbled onto that bunch, he'd be taken care of pronto. Well, I've a prime notion that here may be the end of *Senor* King and some other folks."

"Going to wait for them in here, or outside?" Ord asked.

Hatfield glanced about. "See this shack has another room," he said. "We'll wait in there. I believe I can fix up a little trick that will throw them off their guard and give us a chance to get the drop on them. Chances are there are bunks in that other room. Let's look."

There were bunks in the other room built against the walls and on them were tumbled blankets. Hatfield rolled the blankets together, took them to the other room and hung them in the hangman's nooses. Then he turned the lamp low and surveyed the effect.

"In the dim light they look enough like hanged men to fool jiggers expecting just that," he said. "Before they catch on we'll be on top of them. Now we might as well take it easy. I'd say they won't be back for quite a while and we can hear them coming. Let's see what's in those skillets on the stove. Perhaps we can throw together a surrounding while we wait. All this hell-raising has made me hungry. Did they rope you from the tree, too?"

"That's right," Ord replied, making a wry face. "Durn nigh busted my neck."

"How come you been ridin' up this way?"

Hatfield asked.

"Easy to answer," Ord replied quietly. "Bill Purdy was my buddy. I figured for sure that King killed him. I was out to even up the score. Figured the owlhoot was somewhere in the hills. Then the other day that damn breed he mentioned, he works for Ace Turner, said to me that he heard Bert King was dead and asked if he had a brother who looked like him. I told him I didn't know, but why did he ask. He said he saw a feller up around Sweetwater Canyon who sure looked a heap like Bert King. That was the bait, of course. I rode up this way after dark and found this place. There was nobody around. So I rode back again today hoping to find King. I found him, all right, but didn't get much fun out of it."

Hatfield nodded. "A smart bunch, all right," he said. "Came darn near outsmarting us both."

They found cooked meat in the skillets. There were some dough cakes on the table. They proceeded to eat a hearty meal washed down with numerous cups of coffee. Then they took up positions in the back room where they could keep an eye on the door, and waited for the return of the owlhoots.

The wait was a long one. The tedious minutes dragged into hours. Ord fumed and fidgeted, examining his gun continuously and peering out of the window into the darkness where nothing could be seen. Hatfield reclined comfortably on one of the bunks, drowsing from time to time.

"You might as well take it easy," he told his companion. "I figure they won't get back till around night."

The great clock in the sky wheeled westward. The smell of evening was in the air. As the sun sank, the rimrock was a line of pulsing flame. From down the gorge came the click of approaching hoofs.

Hatfield stood up, stretched his long arms above his head and yawned. He loosened his guns in their sheaths and took up a position just inside the inner door, humming softly under his breath.

"Ain't you got no nerves at all?" demanded Ord in an exasperated whisper.

"Sort of used to this sort of thing and you're not," Hatfield smiled in reply. "You won't have any either when things start. Quiet, now. They're getting close."

The beat of hoofs loudened, then suddenly ceased. Gruff voices sounded outside of the cabin, and there was a creaking of saddle leather and a jingle of bridle irons as men dismounted. The outer door abruptly banged open. Into the room strode Bert

King and his four followers.

"Well, looks like they did for each other, all right," he remarked, glancing at the dangling objects in the dim light. "Turn that lamp up, Hawkins, it's almost out."

Hawkins turned up the wick. The lamp flared brightly. He let out a yell of alarm.

"That's not them — that's just blankets!" he yelped. "What the —"

His voice was drowned by Jim Hatfield's thundered command —

"Elevate!"

Hatfield and Ord stepped from the inner room to face the astounded owlhoots. Ord had a cocked gun in his hand. Hatfield stood with his thumbs hooked over his double cartridge belts.

With a yell of rage and terror, King went for his guns. He was fast. Never in his experience had Jim Hatfield encountered such blinding speed. But the Lone Wolf's gun thundered a split second before King pulled trigger.

King reeled back with a howl of pain, blood spurting from his bullet-slashed hand. His gun thudded to the floor. He whirled, dashed past his companions and out the door.

Craig Ord was shooting as fast as he could pull trigger. The man, Hawkins, went down, drilled dead center. His three companions shot it out to the finish. They shot Hatfield's left sleeve to ribbons, streaked a red graze along one bronzed cheek, nicked Craig Ord in the arm. Then they died, riddled with bullets.

Outside sounded a click of racing hoofs.

"King's gettin' away!" bellowed Ord. "After him!"

Hatfield bounded for the door. His foot came down in a pool of blood, he slipped sideways, fell heavily. Ord, who was also rushing for the door fell over him and the two tangled together trying to get up. By the time Hatfield got outside, even the clicking of hoofs had died away. Hatfield whistled shrilly. A moment later Goldy came dashing from where he had holed up in the brush. Ord had retrieved his own horse from under a nearby lean-to.

But Hatfield made no attempt to mount.

"No use," he told his companion. "He's got a head start and it'll be black dark in another five minutes. He'll make it outside the cleft and there's no telling which way he'll turn. Well, anyhow we thinned out the sidewinders a bit. I want to look those bodies over and then we might as well get back to the camp."

The bodies uncovered nothing of significance, nor did a careful search of the cabin. Finally they shut the door on the grisly occupants, mounted their horses and rode down the cleft to the main canyon.

"Ord," Hatfield cautioned his companion, "don't say anything about what happened. Not to anybody. Our silence may puzzle the hellions."

The other nodded. "I'll get King yet," he declared. "That is if you don't beat me to it, which will be all right with me, just so he's got."

CHAPTER 10

Lane Cardigan was excited and optimistic. For several days the solid granite at which the tunnel crew hammered had been replaced by earth and broken shale, and the work was speeded up in consequence.

"Before night we'll be through," Cardigan exulted. "Then a mile of straight track laying across the valley and one more tunnel, shorter and simpler than this one, and the hills are licked. We're forging ahead of the M & K, Hatfield, I believe we're going to win."

"Maybe," the Lone Wolf conceded. He glanced at the sky as he had been doing frequently for the past few days. A cloud bank was rolling down from the north. Only a narrow streak of blue in the south relieved the monotony of the vast leaden arch.

Shortly after noon, Hatfield and Cardigan entered the tunnel.

They were not alone. Word of the expected breakthrough had gotten around and many townspeople were present to witness the event. Among them Hatfield noticed the tall, handsome owner of the Red Cow Saloon, Ace Turner.

Turner spotted them and came over. "Want to offer my congratulations," he said to Cardigan. "You're going to win your fight. This is quite a day, Mr. Cardigan.

"And," he added with a grin, "tomorrow will be quite a day for me. Payday, isn't it?"

"That's right," Cardigan agreed. "The boys should have quite a bust. No work tomorrow. They've earned a day off and a mite of diversion."

"Won't be no diversion for me," grunted Deputy Scarlet, who had drawn near and overheard the conversation. "For me it means work. There'll be more hell-raisin' in Graham tomorrow than you can shake a stick at. Be plenty for the doctor, too, what with busted heads and the like. Only hope his services as coroner won't be needed."

"Come on," said Cardigan. "They must

be getting mighty close to the breakthrough. Don't want to miss it."

They continued along the damp bore. On either hand and over their heads was a web of temporary shoring to prevent falls of rock and earth. Later this would be replaced by permanent masonry. They reached the point where the protecting shield was shoved forward and the workers were bringing down the last cubic yards of earth and crumbling shale. Sledges thudded, drills chattered, the engines of the steam shovels growled and grumbled. A fretting locomotive was coupled to a string of dump cars that carried off the debris as fast as they were loaded to capacity. Everywhere was a scene of cheerful activity. The workers had entered into the spirit of the occasion and each tried to outdo the other as they forged ahead at top speed.

Suddenly a cheer went up from the foremost laborers. Through the crumbling barrier showed a gleam of light. Five more minutes and a flood of sunshine poured through a widening opening. As though in respect for the achievement, a rift had appeared in the overhead cloud bank and through it funneled a beam of golden radiance. The workers cheered louder than ever and were joined by the crowding spectators.

Swiftly the opening was widened and shaped. Riggers raised and bolted into place the great squared timbers of the shoring. The shield edged forward, the supporting beams following its steel lip. The dump train rumbled back with its heaped cars. Track workers crowded forward to hastily lay a few lengths of rail beyond the tunnel mouth.

To the accompaniment of deafening cheers, a locomotive chugged forward with great dignity and paused outside the bore. Its pilot pointed westward, pointing across the shallow valley to the further loom of the hills, the last barrier the grim Tontos had to offer.

Hatfield accompanied Cardigan back through the tunnel. The engineer rubbed his hands together complacently as they surveyed the bore by the light of flares. He talked volubly.

"Nothing more to do but replace the wooden shoring with masonry," he said. "It's okay now, but we can't trust timber once heavy trains start going through. The vibration would be too great. And also, there's always the chance of sparks from the locomotive setting fire to the timbers. That stuff is dry, seasoned wood, and oil-soaked to boot. It would burn easily with a draft always pulling through here like it does. If the shoring should give way, we'd have the whole mountain down on our heads and it would be a mess. A lot harder to get through than the original bore. It would keep coming and coming and there would be no end to it. But we can take our time with the masonry. Getting through so the steel can be laid on west was the important thing. We'd have bored from both ends if it had been practicable to get materials over these infernal hills. Well, we're okay now. The night shift will tidy up and take care of odds and ends, and then knock off.

"There'll be no work tomorrow and to-morrow night. As I said, tomorrow is payday and the whole force will be in town for a royal bust. Well, I reckon the boys have earned it. They've sure done themselves proud. A bonus is to be handed out to everybody. Should be quite a night in Graham, tomorrow night."

Hatfield turned his head at a sound behind him. The crowd that was following them through the bore had drawn close. Ace Turner was walking almost at Cardigan's elbow.

Cardigan was still happy and chatty when they got back to the office and sat down for a smoke; but Hatfield was silent and distraught. Finally his mood affected the engineer who also fell silent.

"Hatfield," he said at length, "you don't seem enthusiastic about the way things are going."

"I'm not," Hatfield replied briefly.

The worried look returned to Cardigan's face. "You mean you think we may have more trouble, aside from what's going on over at the bridge?"

"Yes," Hatfield said. "I do."

"But what could happen?" Cardigan asked. "It seems to me that everything else is going smoothly."

"On the surface, yes," Hatfield admitted. "But there are potentialities to be considered. The hellions have a prime opportunity for causing us big trouble, if they take advantage of it."

"What do you mean?"

Hatfield rolled another cigarette before replying. He did not speak until he got it lit and going to his liking. He exhaled a cloud of smoke.

"Remember what you were telling me could happen if a stray spark from a locomotive ignited the shoring in the tunnel?" he said.

"Why, yes," Cardigan replied, "but we'll take all precautions against that until the permanent masonry is in place."

Hatfield nodded. "But," he said, "did you

ever consider that somebody else might have thought of what the results of a fire in the tunnel would be?"

Cardigan wet his lips with the tip of a nervous tongue. "But — but do you believe somebody might think of it?" he quavered.

"I don't know," Hatfield replied, "but I do know this — while you were telling us about it, I caught Ace Turner doing a nice little chore of eavesdropping, and Ace Turner is too damn friendly with Price and Arch Watson to suit me."

Cardigan's jaw dropped. He stared at the Ranger.

"The stage is all set for just such a try," Hatfield went on. "Tomorrow night the tunnel will be deserted. All the boys will be in town having their bust, including my guards, except those stationed at the bridge and the trestle. What's to prevent somebody slipping in that tunnel and setting a nice little fire? With the draft sucking through there like it does, those oil-soaked beams would burn like tinder. Once started, it would be impossible to extinguish the fire. The shoring would burn away and the whole damn mountain would be down on our heads. And, as you said, the former chore of running the bore would be nothing to what we'd be up against. The M & K would win hands down even if we didn't have trouble with the bridge."

"What are we going to do?" Cardigan asked in genuine alarm. "Post guards at the tunnel? I'll take care of that right away." He rose to his feet, but Hatfield held up his hand.

"Wait," he said, "I've got a better notion. If they should try it, they won't send more than two or three men to handle the chore, but you can bet on it that at least one of those men will be a top hand who's in on everything. If we could drop a loop on that jigger, whoever he might be, there's a good chance he'd talk to save his own neck. Then we'd have the low-down on the rest of the sidewinders and could smash the whole business. As it is, we have nothing on anybody. If we could just handle the chore as I've outlined it, I wouldn't have to take the big gamble I figure to take tomorrow. We'd be sitting pretty and nothing to worry about. What do you think?"

"I think," Cardigan said slowly, "that, as usual, you're right. Okay, I'll string along with you, on one condition."

"What's the condition?" Hatfield asked, with a slight smile. He had a pretty good notion what the answer would be.

"That," Cardigan said vigorously, "I go

along with you. I'm damned if I'm going to let you take a chance on getting killed while I'm sitting back in safety. I'm going to be right there with you."

"Okay," Hatfield chuckled. "You may have to dodge lead. It's a salty bunch — but okay. Now we'll plan things."

Graham roared the following day. The pay car boomed into town about mid-morning, and gold soon poured through the barred windows into the eager hands of the workers, who immediately proceeded to spend it in various ways that made for tumult and excitement. Deputy Scarlet was on the watch, as were Cardigan and Jim Hatfield. So were the railroad guards, who began celebrating early in order to appear drunk and tired by nightfall. One by one, they lurched off to bed, declaring their sleepiness to anybody who cared to listen.

At the west tunnel entrance, all was dark and silent. The mouth of the bore yawned emptily, a black shadow among shadows. No sound came from the depths of the bore to indicate that five men — Hatfield, Cardigan, and three of the ablest and most trusted guards — were crouching in the spaces between the shoring timbers, alert and watchful. Just behind the silent watchers, lay a huge bundle of oil-soaked cotton waste.

Slowly, the hours passed. Midnight drew near. "Beginning to look like you figured wrong," Cardigan whispered to Hatfield.

"Take it easy," the Lone Wolf whispered back. "Takes time to ride around the hills and get here. And they wouldn't start till well after dark."

Another hour passed, and suddenly Hatfield whispered a warning. A moment later the others heard it, a faint clicking sound that steadily grew louder — the beat of horses' irons on the hard ground.

The clicking ceased and was followed by a popping of saddle leather and a jingling of bit irons as men dismounted. A light flared up at the tunnel mouth. The forms of three men were visible in the tunnel. They carried large tin containers.

"All right," said a voice that Hatfield vaguely recognized. "All right, drench the lower timbers with the oil. I'll set the light as soon as you finish. Then let the jiggers see if they can dig through tomorrow. Hustle up, we want to get away from here. Strike a light, Cale, and help me unscrew these tops."

The shadowy forms moved to the side walls of the tunnel. Outlined in the glow of a flare was a lean, lanky man Hatfield instantly recognized as Bert King, the renegade cowhand. His heart beat exultantly. King would know plenty, if he could just be made to talk.

King and the others yelled with alarm as a sheet of flame roared up in the dark beyond where they stood, flickering almost to the roof beams, as Lane Cardigan touched a match to the bundle of oil-soaked cotton waste.

"Get your hands up!" Hatfield shouted, standing out in the glow. "Get them up, I say, you're covered."

He had hoped that the arsonists would obey the command — to do otherwise would be rank suicide, with four guns trained on them. Two of the owlhoots started to raise their hands, but with a yell of fury, Bert King went for his gun.

Hatfield shot him, aiming for the left shoulder, but King moved sideways at the instant Hatfield fired. His answering bullet fanned the Ranger's face. Then King crumpled up and fell as his companions, fired by his daring, also tried to get into action, and died under the blazing guns of the guards.

Holstering his Colt, Hatfield walked forward and knelt beside King. The owlhoot, shot through the body just above the heart, was alive but going fast. Hatfield leaned close.

"King," he said, "you're going to take the Big Jump. Come clean and ease your conscience before you die. Tell me who sent you to do this job."

King glared up at him, blood bubbling over his lips.

"Go — to — hell!" he mouthed thickly. "Goddamn you — go — to — hell!"

He rattled in his blood-filled throat. His chest arched mightily, fell in, and did not rise again. His glaring eyes grew fixed and stony.

Hatfield gazed down at the dead owlhoot with respect.

"Bad," he remarked, "bad, mean as a Gila monster, plumb snake-blooded! But he went out like a man! Well, we didn't learn anything, but we saved the tunnel, anyhow. Put out that waste and be sure there are no sparks left lying around. Porter, take up your post at the east end of the tunnel. Cranshaw, you stick here at the west. I don't expect any more trouble tonight, but we'll take no chances. Cardigan, we'd better notify Bob Scarlet and let him take charge of the bodies. This happened on railroad property where we have ample authority, so there'll be no questions asked. Tomorrow we'll have a little showdown."

His eyes were coldly gray as he spoke the last words. Cardigan looked at his set face, and did *not* look forward to tomorrow with unqualified delight.

CHAPTER 11

The following morning there was a definite change for the worse in the weather. The sky was even more deeply gray and the wind that blew out of the north was sharp. It was as if a breath from the prepared grave of the dying year had winged its way to the outer air. Hatfield shook his head.

"Rainy time is getting close," he told Cardigan. "We can look for bad weather most any time now. And it'll hit hardest, per usual, up to the north. Let a good hard rain set in and continue indefinitely and we are in for trouble. I don't like it."

He stood for some moments, eyeing the sky, in his eyes mirrored something of the cold steeliness of the drifting clouds. Abruptly he appeared to arrive at a decision.

"We can't wait any longer," he said. "We've got to move. Are you willing to gamble?"

"Why — why, guess so," Cardigan replied hesitantly. "What do you figure to do?"

"Take over the bridge job and run it as it should be run," Hatfield instantly replied.

"But — but I don't consider myself capable of handling that," Cardigan replied, even more hesitantly.

"You won't have to," Hatfield said. "I'll take Price's place, and handle it."

Cardigan stared at him. Then suddenly his nervous mouth tightened.

"All right," he said. "It may mean my finish, but I'll take a chance."

"Good man!" Hatfield applauded. "Nobody ever got anywhere without taking a chance now and then. And maybe you aren't taking as much a one as you think. Get your horse and let's go! Don't forget what I told you to ask Price. I'd sort of like to hear him explain."

Eastward they rode under the leaden sky with the cold wind whispering sadly through the grasses. Hatfield's face was stern and composed, but Cardigan was distinctly nervous. As they neared the bridge site, his nervousness increased.

"Get a grip on yourself," Hatfield told him harshly. "Nobody's going to shoot you."

Cardigan straightened in his saddle. His mouth tightened. His hands gripped hard on the reins. Jim Hatfield, sure of himself, iron-nerved, unafraid, abruptly experienced a wave of compassion for the slight, stoop-shouldered little man who was going to do his duty in the face of an overwhelming fear. He leaned over and gripped Cardigan's hand in his steely fingers, and his white smile, the smile that men and women found irresistible, lighted his face as if a ray of sunlight had suddenly broken through the lowering storm clouds.

"You'll do," he told Cardigan. "Let's go!"

Up to the bridge they swept at a gallop. The watchful guards patrolling the near bank watched them approach.

"Here it comes!" one remarked in low tones to a companion. "And look at that big hellion's face! I feel sort of sorry for Sime Price."

Dismounting, Hatfield and Cardigan walked out onto the uncompleted span, where Price was standing, directing operations on the building center pier below. His face hardened as he recognized his visitors. He swaggered to meet them.

"Cardigan," he began truculently, "I got a question or two to ask you. I want —"

But Lane Cardigan held up his hand. "Wait a minute, Price," he said, his voice quiet and level, and without a trace of tremor. "Wait, I want to ask *you* a few questions. First off, why are the breakwaters called for in the bridge plans not built or under way?"

Price stared, his jaw dropping slightly. He seemed somewhat taken aback.

"Why — why," he stuttered, "you know those breakwaters are to be built *after* the piers are in."

"Built afterward, hell!" Cardigan exploded. "Do you call yourself an engineer? And what about the piling to provide a solid base for the cribbings? Why haven't they been driven? Why aren't there solid foundations, bedrock, for the anchor piers? Those piers are resting on sand that a little water will turn into quicksand. And those coffer dams! They don't dam anything, and you know it. That is if you are really an engineer and not some incompetent trying to get by on bluff. Which is it, Price? Bluff or plain crookedness?"

Sime Price's face went white, then red. His mouth worked. His eyes blazed.

"Why you blankety-blank squirt!" he roared. "You trying to tell me my business?"

"Yes," Cardigan shot back at him. "No, that's wrong. I'm not *trying* to tell you. I'm *telling* you! Which is it, Price? Bluff or plain double-cross?"

With another roar, Price stepped forward, his huge fists swinging.

"I'll show you which, damn you!" he shouted. One ponderous fist raised to strike. He launched a blow that would have hurled the little engineer into the river, had it landed.

But it didn't land. With the gliding swiftness of a mountain lion, Jim Hatfield was between the pair. Before it had traveled six inches, the blow was blocked, and blocked with an effortless ease that made Price look ridiculous.

"Take it easy," Hatfield cautioned. "You won't settle this by throwing fists."

Price went into a more towering rage.

"You infernal range tramp!" he yelled. "So you are back of this, eh? Well, I'll take care of you."

He paused, gasping with the anger that took his breath away. Hatfield spoke, his voice mild.

"Price," he said, "can you swim?"

The engineer gaped at him in astonishment.

"Sure I can swim! What the hell —" His voice began rising again.

"Then swim!" Hatfield snapped at him. "Clean to Mexico, if you know what's good for you!" His hands shot out, gripped Price, shook him as a terrier shakes a rat, until his teeth rattled in his head. Then, despite the other's frantic struggles, Hatfield lifted him as if he were a child and hurled him off the span and into the river.

Price landed with a mighty splash and disappeared in the muddy water. He broke surface, uttered a strangled yell and headed for the bank, trying to swim and swear at the same time. Hatfield strolled leisurely toward the end of the pier.

"Didn't I tell you it would be worth watchin'?" said one of the guards to his companion.

"It ain't over yet," the other replied. "Price is comin' out full of fight."

"He won't be over full before long," the first speaker predicted.

Price reached dry ground and came swarming up the bank, dripping water and spewing profanity. Hatfield stood calmly waiting. Price topped the bank, paused for a moment to catch his breath, and rushed.

Hatfield hit him left and right. Price shot through the air and landed on his back. He bounded to his feet like a rubber ball, and rushed again, arms flailing. Again Hatfield met him with solid blows. But Price held a better footing this time. He reeled, but did not fall. Ducking his head he charged.

Price was a big man, not so tall, but pounds heavier than the lean Ranger. Although Hatfield landed again with both hands, the very weight of the engineer's rush hurled him back a step or two. He recovered his balance and the two stood toe to toe, slugging it out. There was blood on both faces now. A glancing blow had opened a cut on Hatfield's cheek.

A cheering, yelling crowd surrounded the battlers. Those on Hatfield's side were watchful and alert, ready to discourage with rifle butts any effort at interference. But the bridge workers were strictly neutral and were enjoying themselves hugely.

There was a wild flurry of blows thudding against the flesh. A sudden sharp crack as Hatfield's right fist whipped over with all his two hundred pounds of sinewy muscular power behind it. Price reeled, staggered blindly and fell on his face. He rolled over, gasping and groaning, and trying unsuccessfully to rise. He finally managed to prop his sagging body up on one elbow. He glared at the man who had whipped him, gulped some breath into his laboring lungs and lurched painfully to his feet. With another glare he headed for his office and quarters in a shack built near the river bank.

"Don't go for a gun, Price," Hatfield

warned. "If you do, it'll be the last one you ever lay hands on."

Price turned to shake his fist and swear. Hatfield strode toward him, face bleak, eyes coldly gray. Price backed up hurriedly, holding his hands before his bloody face.

"You got one hour, Price, to pack up and get out," the Lone Wolf told him. "Don't be here when the hour is up, unless you want a month's stay in a hospital."

"I ain't finished with you yet, damn you," Price replied. Muttering under his breath, he turned again and lurched into the shack. One of the mounted guards casually sidled his horse over to block the door.

"Don't aim for no shootin' in the back," he observed.

Hatfield was not particularly worried about that, but he nodded his appreciation.

"Come on," he told the white and speechless Cardigan, "we got work to do." His voice rose in a shout — "Maloney!"

The big stonework boss came forward, a grin on his face.

"Yes, *Sor!*"

"Maloney," Hatfield said, "you're in charge here now, under my orders. We've got work to do. There's bad weather coming, and if flood water catches us before we're ready for it, we're sunk. Send a gang into the woods over there and have them cut and trim piles. I want fifty-foot lengths. Have another gang assemble that pile driver and get it going. We're driving piles around the anchor piers and building cribbing on them to support the spans. Then we'll excavate under the piers and drop them to bedrock, where they'll be properly foundationed. Build a coffer dam around that central pier and start pumping. If you know your job, you can get out the sand and drop that pier to bedrock, too. Start laying stone on top the pier at the same time. You can do that, too, if you know your job. If you don't, I'll show you how!"

"I know me job, Sor," growled Maloney. "You give the orders, I'll carry 'em out. By God, it's sure foine to be workin' for a *man* again!"

"There goes Price," Cardigan told Hatfield nervously, pointing to a horseman riding swiftly south along the river bank. "I'm afraid we haven't finished with him, Hatfield. He isn't going to Graham. He's heading for Sierra, the county seat, or I'm much mistaken. I've a notion he'll be back."

"We'll be here if he does," Hatfield replied briefly.

CHAPTER 12

The gray dusk of twilight brought torrential rains, and a long awaited message, coming by special train, from Jaggers Dunn in New York. Dunn's message was brief and to the point:

"To all officers and employees of the C & P Railroad System: Orders issued by the bearer of this letter, J. J. Hatfield, are to be obeyed without question, without delay, and to the fullest extent."

Hatfield read the message as darkness descended.

The night was black. The rain fell harder and harder. Louder and louder sounded the angry growl of the rising river. It provided an eerie undertone for the roar and thunder of the pile driver, the chattering of crane engines, the thud of mauls and the unceasing creak of the jack levers. High in the leaden heavens, the cold wind wailed, swooping to earth in mighty gusts that drove the level lances of the rain before them.

In the lurid glow of the flares, the superstructure of the bridge stood out — the bloody bones of a newly fleshed skeleton. The ponderous horizontal girders stretching out over the swirling water were stiffened arms with hands chopped off at the wrists. The tall towers were crowned with writhing shadow-mists, the supporting cables slanting downward through the gloom like the anchor threads of some monstrous spider web.

And beneath the web of steel the tireless workers seemed frantic flies struggling amid the meshes.

The turbulent night wore on. Midnight approached. Hatfield and Cardigan were snatching a bite to eat and some steaming coffee in the cooking shanty on the east bank.

Suddenly the door banged open, letting in a swirling gust of rain-laden wind. A wild-eyed man stood outlined against the dark.

"The pier's slidin'!" he shouted. "Maloney says it's already more than an inch downstream and an inch out of plumb!"

Hatfield and Cardigan leaped to their feet and rushed out of the shanty. At the pier all was confusion and shouting. The jacks had ceased their infinitesimally slow rise, for the span had been lifted to the required height. Great timbers, the final supporting beams of the crib, swung from the derrick chains.

The operators gripped their levers and waited.

Hatfield's voice rose and stilled the tumult.

"We've got to get those timbers into place before she slides off balance," he said, after he had gotten quiet.

The workers stared at him. Not a man there failed to realize what it would mean to be caught in the cribbing if the tremendous weight of the pier slipped and toppled. A bloody pulp would take the place of what had been a man.

"I'm not assigning anybody to the chore," Hatfield's quiet voice resumed. "I'm handling it myself, but I'll need one more man to swing the other end of the timbers. I'm asking for volunteers."

With cheers and shouts, men began crowding forward, but big Maloney shouldered them aside.

"I'm foreman here!" roared the giant mason. "If the Big Boss is takin' over this job, begorra, Tim Maloney is takin' over with him! Let's go, Sor, we ain't got no time to waste."

Stripped to the waist, they descended between the stonework and the walls of the crib, standing on prepared supports bolted to the crib timbers. Bolts and mauls lay ready to hand.

"Lower away!" Hatfield thundered above the river's roar.

The derrick engine chattered, the huge, meticulously squared and shaped timber descended, swung over to the crib wall. Hatfield reached out and gripped one end of the stick by the bolt holes. Slowly, steadily, with terrific effort he swung the timber over and fitted it between the upmost crib beam and the bottom of the span. The derrick engine snarled slowly as the operator eased off with infinite care. The far end of the beam swung within Maloney's reach. Now came the most ticklish part of the chore — the balancing of the timber and casting off the derrick chain. Hatfield accomplished it, and they began working the timber into place.

It was precision work to the ultimate, for only a fraction of an inch of space was left between the beam and the span. Great muscles stood out like ropes on Hatfield's back, arms, and shoulders. The salt of sweat on his lips was dashed away by the driving sheets of rain. He and Maloney strained and tugged. They were doing the work usually performed by a gang of six brawny bridge builders.

Beneath them sounded a muffled creaking

and groaning as the stonework of the pier rocked and shifted on the disintegrating sand bed. The crib timbers cracked and shivered as the river beat against and tore at the piling upon which the timbers rested.

At last the beam was in place. Thick bolts were pounded into the slanting holes bored and joined with the utmost nicety. Ten minutes more of heart-breaking effort and the timber was firmly in place. But three more beams remained.

The mighty struggle was repeated on the far side of the crib, to the accompaniment of an ever loudening protest from the tortured masonry of the pier.

Gasping for breath, red flashes storming before their eyes, Hatfield and Maloney rested for a few moments. Then they tackled the third timber, and the one farthest from the shore.

Now the difficulty of the task increased, for the ends of the beam had to be fitted between the sides of the right-angled beams already in place. The derrick engine jigged and sputtered. The operator played his levers as a master organist plays a keyboard. Hatfield and Maloney tugged and strained and swore. But finally the support was in place and securely bolted to its fellows.

"One more," Hatfield called cheerily to

his companion. "We'll make it, feller."

"Maybe," Maloney roared back, "but she's movin', Sor, I can feel it."

"Lower away!" Hatfield bellowed.

The derrick engine boomed and chattered. The cables creaked, the chains jangled. Down through the flickering light swung the remaining stick. It halted, poised, moved sideways with infinite slowness, came to a pause, level with and only inches away from the gap between the span and its support. Hatfield seized his end, swung it into place. Thrusting his skinned and bleeding fingers into the bolt holes, he grimly held on while Maloney jockeyed his end toward the narrow opening.

With a whoop of triumph, Maloney swung the beam into place. His exultant shout changed to a yell of alarm.

"The pier's shifted," he howled. "Moved three inches that time. Another slip and we're done."

"No time to bolt this stick in place!" Hatfield shouted back. "Hang onto the bolt holes and hold it for the span!"

His voice rolled forth, drowning all other sounds —

"Cardigan! Ease off on the jacks! Sift sand, feller, sift sand!"

The hydraulic jacks began to click as iron-hard muscles worked them at frantic speed. Slowly, slowly, its movement imperceptible to the eye, the span began to sink. Hatfield and Maloney, leaning far back against the trembling stonework of the sliding pier, held the stick in place with the strength of desperation.

While the jack levers clicked and Cardigan's encouraging shouts boomed from the shore, Hatfield held on.

Abruptly the clicking and the shouting ceased. From the cribbing sounded a groaning and rumbling, which also abruptly ceased. Then, above the roar of the dashing water and the hiss of the rain came Cardigan's triumphant yell, followed by a thunder of cheering.

With a gasp of relief, Hatfield let his numb arms drop to his side. He knew what that meant. The weight was off the jack heads and transferred to the crib. The jacks had been hurled aside and now the mighty mass of the span was anchoring the piles to bedrock.

"We did it, Sor!" shouted Maloney, "somethin' that's niver been done before in the history of bridge buildin', or I miss me guess."

With a few maul strokes, they drove the bolts into place. Then they climbed swiftly from the death trap in which they had spent the past two hours, for there was still a chance of the pier slipping a little more, although now no serious damage could be done.

"I really believe we got it licked," Hatfield told Cardigan as he rested in the cooking shanty. "No matter how much more the river rises, it will rise slowly, and we're safe against that. A few more days, at the rate we're going, and the piers themselves will be bedrocked and built up to take the weight of the bridge. And with the breakwaters upstream functioning properly, no conceivable volume of water could cause anything to worry about.

"All right, now, you take it easy. I'm going out to see if my guards are on the job. I still got a sort of jumpy feeling that we're not finished with Watson and his bunch."

CHAPTER 13

Hatfield kept the guards constantly on the alert.

"I don't know what could happen, but we're taking no chances," he told them. "We're up against a bad bunch that will stop at nothing."

And then the totally unexpected happened. In the gray light of the dawn, a wild-eyed horseman stormed down to the bridge.

"Where's Hatfield?" he yelled, sliding from his reeking saddle.

"All hell's busted loose," he told the Ranger. "About fifty sidewinders swooped down on our camp there where they dammed the crick. Crane Ballard was with 'em, and Ace Turner, and that fat lawyer fellow Watson from over to Sierra. They caught the boys settin'. They're buildin' up that dam again, buildin' it high, and openin' the channel to the river. They aim to back up that crick and send it hellin' down here to wash out the bridge."

Lane Cardigan swore explosively, but Hatfield only asked in quiet tones, "How did you get away, Walt?"

"I was out on the river bank," the guard explained. "One of us always stayed out there, like you ordered. It was dark and they didn't see me. The rest of the boys were asleep under the lean-to. I saw everything that went on. I couldn't get to our broncs, but when they all got busy on the dam, I managed to steal one of their horses and slide away. They didn't see me."

"When did they hit the camp?" Hatfield asked.

"Right after midnight. It took me quite a

spell to get a chance at the horse."

Hatfield called his guards and in terse sentences explained what had happened.

"We're riding up there pronto," he told them. "If we don't stop the hellions before they finish that dam and blow it, everything we've done here will go for nothing."

The guards stared at him.

"But, Cap," one said, "you know us fellers ain't got no authority off the railroad. If it comes to a shootin' and somebody gets hurt, we may be in for big trouble."

"You'll have all the authority you need," Hatfield replied briefly. He was fumbling at a cunningly concealed secret pocket in his broad leather belt. He raised his hand to his shirt front. When he dropped it, there was pinned to his shirt a gleaming silver star set on a silver circle, the feared and honored badge of the Texas Rangers!

Hatfield's voice rang out. "I'm deputizing you as citizens of the State of Texas to assist me in the prevention of a crime," he told them. "Let's go."

There was a moment of silence, then somebody shouted —

"Good gosh! He's a Ranger!"

"Yeah," whooped another voice, "A Texas Ranger! I got him spotted at last. A Texas Ranger, and — *The Lone Wolf!*"

187

A babble of exclamations arose. Men stared at the almost legendary figure whose exploits were the talk of the Southwest.

Lane Cardigan swore feebly. Big Maloney grinned to split his red face.

"All right," Hatfield repeated, as he led Goldy from under his shelter and swung into the saddle, "let's go!"

Through the rain and the wind they rode, Goldy setting the pace. Hatfield's eyes were as coldly gray as the lowering sky overhead, his face as bleak as the granite hills. Mile after speeding mile they rode, with the wind moaning in the sky and the angry river roaring in its rocky bed. The possemen were silent and grimly determined.

They topped a final ridge and the building dam lay before them. Under the busy hands of a swarm of workers the masonry had already risen to a respectable height. The channel to the river had been dredged out.

In front of the workings stood a score of men with levelled rifles. A little to one side were Arch Watson, Ace Turner and a tall, broad-shouldered man Hatfield deduced must be Crane Ballard.

"Hold up!" Watson shouted. "That's close enough. Any closer and we'll blow you from your hulls!"

Hatfield halted the posse. "No shooting unless I give the word," he cautioned. "Most of those fellers there are just hired hands. I don't want any of them hurt if we can avoid it."

He swung from the saddle and strode steadily forward, heedless of the threatening rifles. His hands swung loosely at his sides. On his broad chest glittered the star of the Rangers.

"I tell you to hold up!" howled Watson. "Don't come a step closer!"

Hatfield kept on walking. Suddenly his voice rolled in thunder above the beat of the rain and the noise of the river —

"In the name of the State of Texas! Throw down those guns, disperse, and go about your business in an orderly manner. This is an unlawful assemblage!"

There was a moment of silence. It was broken by a clang of metal as a big fellow at the end of the line let his rifle fall to the ground.

"You fellers can do as you please," he shouted, "but me, I'm quittin'. I ain't buckin' no Texas Rangers, pertickler not that one."

He turned and strode away. Behind him other rifles clattered to the ground. The line melted and was gone, leaving Ballard, Turner and Watson standing alone.

Hatfield's voice rang out again —

"Crane Ballard, Ace Turner, and Arch Watson, I arrest you for the murder of Tobe Harness and Bill Purdy. Anything you say —"

Ace Turner let out a scream of rage and terror.

"Get him, Arch! Get him! I told you he knew!" he yelled, hands streaking to his guns.

Hatfield's hands flashed down and up. The workers on the dam scattered wildly as the guns blazed and thundered.

A moment later, Jim Hatfield lowered his smoking Colts and gazed at the two figures sprawled on the ground. A red streak showed on one of Hatfield's bronzed cheeks. Blood dripped from his bullet-creased left hand. But he stood firm and erect and turned his gaze on Crane Ballard who was cowering against the stone work of the uncompleted dam, shaking in every limb, his face ghastly white.

Hatfield holstered his guns and walked slowly forward. Ballard shrank away from the Lone Wolf's terrible eyes.

"I didn't do it!" he screamed. "I never meant — I never intended — I never ordered any killings. They did it on their own."

"Ballard," Hatfield said, "for years you've skirted the edge of the law, stepping over a mite now and then, but never quite enough to enable anybody to drop a loop on you. This time you've tangled your twine. You're just as guilty as those two sidewinders there on the ground."

Crane Ballard raised a trembling hand to his ghastly, twitching face.

"I tell you I didn't have anything to do with it," he yammered. "They got out of hand. I couldn't control them."

"Ballard," Hatfield pursued relentlessly, "you started this thing. Because of your scheming and manipulating, men have died. You rode a crooked trail, and now it's trail's end."

The railroad president was reduced to a gibbering, palsied wreck. He sagged against the stone work, mouthing his words, uttering only incoherencies.

"I never ordered them to kill anybody," he managed to moan at last. "I just hired them to hold up the C & P so we could reach the pass through the Tontos first."

Hatfield gazed steadily at him.

"Ballard," he said, "I believe you when you say you never ordered any killings, but you'd have one awful time making a jury believe it. I'm going to give you a chance, a chance to make some slight amends for what you've done.

"Get back to your railroad. Build it as it should be built, and operate it as it should be operated. The country up there needs it. That's the only reason I'm giving you a chance. No more interfering with the C & P project. We'll let you build. We won't keep you out of the pass through the Diablos. But the C & P goes through first, even if you get there with your steel before we do. And keep your nose clean, Ballard, or you'll end up dancing on nothing or making hair bridles for the state the rest of your life. Don't forget, you've made admissions before fifty witnesses. Now get going!"

Ballard got going, a broken man, his shoulders hunched forward. After him followed his guards and his workers, with many a fearful glance back at the motionless forms lying in the rain.

"Well, I reckon that settles that," Hatfield observed as the last horse disappeared in the rain mists. "All right, back to the bridge. We got work to do. Should set that middle span into place before the end of the week."

As they rode south, Cardigan drew up beside Hatfield.

"Well," he remarked, "as you said, that sort of settles that. You sure did Ballard up brown. The way he crawled was something to see. I don't think he'll ever cause anybody trouble any more. He looked like an old man when he rode away."

"I largely used bluff on him," Hatfield chuckled. "Didn't give him time to stop and think that the only two who could really witness against him were lying dead at his feet. I just kept prodding him until he made admissions that would convict him of plenty if he ever came to trial, though doubtless not for murder. I agree with you. I don't think we'll have any more trouble with Ballard. And the hellions really responsible for the killing of Harness and the others paid off in full."

"How did you know Turner and Watson were responsible for the killings?" Cardigan asked.

Hatfield chuckled again. Despite the wind and the rain, he deftly rolled and lighted a cigarette.

"Good deal of bluff there, too," he replied. "I had very little on them. Wouldn't have wanted to risk such evidence before a jury. A smart lawyer would mighty likely have picked it to pieces. I knew for sure, in my own mind, that Ace Turner killed Harness, although he never intended to do Harness in. He was after me. When poor Tobe showed on Goldy, Turner, who was holed up in that thicket waiting his chance, recognized the horse and figured I was forking him."

"How did you know Turner did it?"

"Turner was smart, but not quite smart enough," Hatfield replied. "He covered his regular clothes with overalls, put on a set of false whiskers. You see, his notion was to let folks see him riding along the trail, after the killing, and set them looking for a killer with black whiskers. I got suspicious of that in a hurry. I felt sure the real killer didn't grow whiskers. But where Turner slipped bad was in not changing his boots after he slid into town."

"How's that?"

Hatfield pinched out his cigarette butt and cast it aside.

"The earth in that thicket was damp, black mud," he explained. "Quite different from the surface of the trail, or anything around town. The trail was dusty, and so were the streets of Graham, but under the thick chaparral growth, the earth had remained quite damp since the last rain. When I saw Turner in the Red Cow the night of the day Harness was killed, his boots had black mud on the heels."

Cardigan whistled.

"Don't miss anything, do you?" he said.

"I was already suspicious of Turner," Hatfield resumed. In a few brief sentences he recounted the attempt of his life in the hills the day after the dynamiting of the machine shop.

"I spotted that sidewinder as a man who talked with Turner just before Doc Horton made his try for me," he explained. "The slip of paper I took from his pocket was undoubtedly a waiter's check for food and drinks he had consumed. And somebody other than the waiter who tallied the bill, doubtless the proprietor of the place, had written the word 'roof' at the bottom of the sheet. Well, a roof is on the house, and the word 'roof' written on a bill signifies that the food and drinks are on the house."

"I see," exclaimed Cardigan, "and then you had me work Turner into okaying the bill I ran up, and the handwriting on the two were the same."

"That's right," Hatfield nodded, "and pretty well proved what I suspected, that the drygulcher was in cahoots with Turner. But the best lead I had on Turner was an exploded cartridge I picked up in the thicket from which Harness was drygulched. It was a thirty-thirty shell, an unusual calibre for this section. I wide-looped Turner's rifle from his office, and it was thirty-thirty calibre. That mighty nigh to tied Turner up with the killing."

Hatfield paused to roll another cigarette.

"My ace-in-the-hole, though," he said, "was that Turner and Watson didn't know for sure how much I had on them, and a guilty conscience made them scairt I knew more than I really did. So Turner went off half-cocked and tipped their hand. Turner was a vicious killer but not much else. Watson was the brains of the outfit. Watson, of course, figured to take over the M & K once he got Ballard properly in hand. Ballard figured Watson was his man, but in truth, Ballard was Watson's man, although Ballard didn't know it. Watson read him right and played on his failings. Ballard set up to be a salty hombre, but Watson knew at the bottom he was weak and was not the killer type. So he set to work to get Ballard in so deep he would have to agree to anything Watson proposed. But Turner fumbled the deal and let all three of them in for a showdown without a full hand."

"And that settles that," Cardigan repeated.

"Yes," Hatfield nodded. "I'll have Bob Scarlet drop over to the hospital and pay Doc Horton a little visit. Horton, despite his gun slinging record, is another weak member, and his tie-up with Turner and Watson is well known. He'll talk to save his own hide and give Scarlet a line on the shorthorns of the bunch that are still mavericking around. Bob will take care of them. Yes, it about winds up my Ranger chore over here, but I can't very well drag my rope till that darn bridge is in shape."

A week later, Hatfield, Cardigan and Tim Maloney stood and watched the center span of the great bridge lowered into place. Firm and solid, based on eternal bedrock, the massive piers stood. The breakwaters were completed, shunting the force of the current between the piers. Maloney had already removed his cribbings and coffer dams.

The instant the center span was dropped into place, a swarm of workers got busy with bolts and rivets. Trackmen spaced ties and spiked down rails. A cheer rose as the last spike was hammered into place.

Hatfield glanced at his watch.

"Just in time," he chuckled, "here she comes. Line up the switch from the trestle and to the bridge," he shouted.

An answering shout came from across the river. A switch-stand target changed color, even as the wail of a whistle, faint with distance, sounded.

All eyes turned to the east. Speeding

toward the bridge was a giant passenger locomotive. Behind it rolled a long green-and-gold splendor with WINONA stencilled on its sides.

A few minutes later the C & P General Manager's private car rumbled across the span and came to a hissing halt beside where Jim Hatfield and his companions stood.

Down the steps came a stocky, broad-shouldered old man. He was hatless and his glorious mane of crinkly white hair swept back from his big dome-shaped forehead. There was a smile in his frosty blue eyes. He held out his hand to Hatfield.

"Hello, Jim," he greeted. "Everything under control, I see, per usual."

He nodded pleasantly to the others.

"Come into the car and tell me about it," he invited Hatfield. "See you boys in a little while," he told Cardigan and Maloney.

Some fifteen or twenty minutes later, Hatfield stepped out onto the platform.

"Come in, Lane," he called to Cardigan. "Bring Maloney along. He wants to see you both."

"Hear you're doing a fine job out here, Cardigan," said the General Manager as he shook hands. "Keep it up. Drive on through the Diablos and on to Franklin as fast as you can. We can use you down around the Gulf when you finish this chore.

"And this is Maloney, eh?" he greeted the boss mason. "Wainwright," he called to his secretary, "come here and meet *Mr.* Maloney, who will be the new line's chief for maintenance."

Cardigan thanked the General Manager, heartily. Both Dunn and Hatfield felt that Maloney would have liked to say something appropriate, if he only knew how. But all the big fellow finally managed to stutter was —

"G-g-good gosh!"

General Manager Dunn turned to Hatfield. "When you coming in with us, Jim?" he asked. "There's a prime job waiting for you whenever you feel like taking over."

But Hatfield's gaze was on the western hill tops. He smiled and shook his head.

"Reckon I have a job, sir," he replied. "I'll be riding now. Captain Bill will have another little chore lined up for me by the time I get back to the post."

They watched him ride away, tall and graceful atop his great golden horse, the sunlight etching his sternly handsome profile in flame, to where duty called and new adventure waited. And as he turned in his saddle to wave goodbye, glorious in his youth and strength, the frosty eyes of the old General Manager were wistful. Perhaps because of his own lined face and snowy hair, and the knowledge that the Eternal Trail End that once had seemed so far away now was "just beyond."

Or perhaps because, long years ago, before he dreamed of the C & P Railroad, Jaggers Dunn had himself been a rider of the purple sage.

ABOUT THE AUTHOR

Leslie Scott was born in Lewisburg, West Virginia. During the Great War, he joined the French Foreign Legion and spent four years in the trenches. In the 1920s he worked as a mining engineer and bridge builder in the western American states and in China before settling in New York. A barroom discussion in 1934 with Leo Margulies, who was managing editor for Standard Magazines, prompted Scott to try writing fiction. He went on to create two of the most notable series characters in Western pulp magazines. In 1936, Standard Magazines launched, and in *Texas Rangers,* Scott under the house name of **Jackson Cole** created Jim Hatfield, Texas Ranger, a character whose popularity was so great with readers that this magazine featuring his adventures lasted until 1958. When others eventually began contributing Jim Hatfield stories, Scott created another Texas Ranger hero,

Walt Slade, better known as *El Halcon,* the Hawk, whose exploits were regularly featured in *Thrilling Western.* In the 1950s Scott moved quickly into writing book-length adventures about both Jim Hatfield and Walt Slade in long series of original paperback Westerns. At the same time, however, Scott was also doing some of his best work in hardcover Westerns published by Arcadia House; thoughtful, well-constructed stories, with engaging characters and authentic settings and situations. Among the best of these, surely, are *Silver City* (1953), *Longhorn Empire* (1954), *The Trail Builders* (1956), and *Blood on the Rio Grande* (1959). In these hardcover Westerns, many of which have never been reprinted, Scott proved himself highly capable of writing traditional Western stories with characters who have sufficient depth to change in the course of the narrative and with a degree of authenticity and historical accuracy absent from many of his series stories.

We hope you have enjoyed this Large Print book. Other Thorndike, Wheeler, and Chivers Press Large Print books are available at your library or directly from the publishers.

For information about current and upcoming titles, please call or write, without obligation, to:

Publisher
Thorndike Press
295 Kennedy Memorial Drive
Waterville, ME 04901
Tel. (800) 223-1244

or visit our Web site at:

www.gale.com/thorndike
www.gale.com/wheeler

OR

Chivers Large Print
published by BBC Audiobooks Ltd
St James House, The Square
Lower Bristol Road
Bath BA2 3SB
England
Tel. +44(0) 800 136919
email: bbcaudiobooks@bbc.co.uk
www.bbcaudiobooks.co.uk

All our Large Print titles are designed for easy reading, and all our books are made to last.